Ellis Peters is the pseudonym of Edith Pargeter, the distinguished author of many historical novels, including the *Heaven Tree Trilogy* and *The Marriage of Meggotta* (available from Futura). As Ellis Peters she also writes the bestselling Brother Cadfael mysteries. She lives in Shropshire.

Also by Ellis Peters in Futura:

Brother Cadfael Mysteries
A MORBID TASTE FOR BONES
ONE CORPSE TOO MANY
MONK'S-HOOD
SAINT PETER'S FAIR
THE LEPER OF SAINT GILES
THE VIRGIN IN THE ICE
THE SANCTUARY SPARROW
THE DEVIL'S NOVICE
DEAD MAN'S RANSOM
THE PILGRIM OF HATE
AN EXCELLENT MYSTERY
THE RAVEN IN THE FOREGATE
THE ROSE RENT
THE HERMIT OF EYTON FOREST
THE CONFESSION OF BROTHER HALUIN
THE HERETIC'S APPRENTICE
THE POTTER'S FIELD

THE FIRST CADFAEL OMNIBUS
(A MORBID TASTE FOR BONES, ONE CORPSE
TOO MANY, MONK'S-HOOD)

THE SECOND CADFAEL OMNIBUS
(SAINT PETER'S FAIR, THE LEPER OF SAINT
GILES, THE VIRGIN IN THE ICE)

Inspector Felse Mysteries
A NICE DERANGEMENT OF EPITAPHS
BLACK IS THE COLOUR OF MY TRUE
LOVE'S HEART
THE KNOCKER ON DEATH'S DOOR
RAINBOW'S END
FALLEN INTO THE PIT
DEATH AND THE JOYFUL WOMAN

Ellis Peters writing as Edith Pargeter

The Heaven Tree Trilogy
THE HEAVEN TREE
THE GREEN BRANCH
THE SCARLET SEED

THE MARRIAGE OF MEGOTTA

ELLIS PETERS

The
GRASS
WIDOW'S
TALE

Futura

A Futura Book

First published in Great Britain in 1968
by Collins Publishers Ltd

This edition published in 1991 by Futura Publications
A Division of Macdonald & Co (Publishers) Ltd
London & Sydney

ISBN 0 7088 4995 4

Printed and bound in Great Britain by
BPCC Hazell Books
Aylesbury, Bucks, England
Member of BPCC Ltd.

Futura Publications
A Division of
Macdonald & Co (Publishers) Ltd
165 Great Dover Street
London SE1 4YA

A member of Maxwell Macmillan Publishing Corporation

CHAPTER I

THE DAY BEFORE her birthday turned out to be a dead loss right from the start. It dawned reluctantly in murk, like a decrepit old man with a hangover half-opening one gummy eye, to glare sickly at the world and recoil into misanthropy. Morose commuters groped their way through a gloom that did not lift. Slimy black mud picked up by the set-back heels of the new season's shoes spattered mini-skirted legs to the thigh with miniature cow-pats, which dried greenish-grey and clung like glue. Desultory moisture in the air, balanced irritatingly between rain and mist, caused half of the hurrying morning tide to open their umbrellas, while leaving the other half unconvinced, and to walk the length of the street was to witness the formation of two inimical factions. There was no letter from Dominic in the post, nothing but a dismal circular for a furniture sale and a quarterly gas bill, first delayed and then wantonly inflated by a perverse computer. It was impossible to do the housework without switching on lights, and the spectral world outside the misted windows instantly sank deeper into the all-defiling ooze of dirt and darkness. There was no real daylight all that day.

When October turns traitor it can sometimes outdo the worst of the winter in nastiness. By the time George came home, late in the afternoon, it was raining with a restrained malice that wet people through before they realised it, and yet did nothing to rinse the spattered shop-windows and greasy pavements. All the lights were hazed with condensation and clinging filth; the day was a write-off, and the night already settling malevolently over Comerford.

Bunty heard the car slurp dejectedly along the kerb and slow to turn in at the gate; and her heart rose so violently that only then did she realise with a shock how low it had

5

sunk. George was home, there would be a letter from Dominic in the morning. She examined with astonishment, and rejected with disdain, the feeling that she had been for some hours utterly alone.

And George came in, tall and tired, stained with the greyness of the day, and said, so abruptly that she knew he was hardly with her at all: "Pitch a few things in a case for me, will you? I've got to go down to London." Some sense of guilt touched him vaguely through the cloud of his abstraction. "I'm sorry!" he said. "Something's come up."

Bunty had been a detective's wife for just over twenty years. Her responses were as nearly automatic as made ⁊ matter. You do not send your husband out on a job with a divided mind; least of all do you claim any part of his concentration for yourself when he needs it all intact for his own purposes. She closed her magazine briskly, crossed to him and kissed him with the brevity of old custom.

"Got time for tea? Ready in five minutes. What difference can that make?"

"You don't mind?" he said, tightening his arm round her for a moment. His voice was weary; so were his eyes. The Midshire C.I.D. were having no easy time this autumn, and there wasn't much Bunty didn't know, directly or indirectly, about their preoccupations.

"I mind like hell!" Since when had they dealt in polite, accommodating lies? "But there it is. You get something good out of it, and I'll be satisfied. Anything promising?"

"Hard to say. It might be a break-through, it might just drop dead. You know how it is."

She knew just how it was; usually it dropped dead. But they had to pursue it just the same, as long as there was breath in it. "It's time you had a break. Is it the wage-snatch? Has something broken there?"

"No, the fur job. If we're lucky it might turn out to be something. They've picked up a small floating operator on another charge, one of the possibles we had listed. Specialises in driving jobs, anything on wheels, especially get-away cars. He answers to one of the two descriptions we got out of the driver of that van, but not any better than a dozen other professionals do. The thing is, he produced an alibi for the time of our job, but as soon as they probed it, it fell down. There may be nothing in it. Maybe his own gang want him shopped, for some reason of their own. Anyhow, they don't want to know about him, and he's left wide open. It may be the moment to get something out of him, or there may be nothing to get. But we've got to try it."

"Of course! I hope it turns out right, I hope he's your man. You sit down," she said, steering him backwards into his own chair by the fire, "and I'll put the kettle on. By the time I've packed it'll be boiling. How long will you have to be away?"

"I don't know, maybe two or three days. If I do get a lead, it'll be down there I shall have to follow it up. I told Duckett, this is some metropolitan gang moving out. I'm sure of it. Distances have shrunk since we got the motorways, and town's getting too congested and too hot. The pickings are better out here. And we're beginners," he said grimly. "They know where the pastures are green, all right! And the police greener!"

"They think!" said Bunty from the kitchen. The gas hissed under the kettle, and the busy, contented purr of water heating began almost at once. "You're taking the car?" she asked.

"It's quicker, and I need to be mobile. I shall have to fill up on the way out. Thank the lord, at least it isn't foggy."

"I'd better reckon on three days or so, then? Keep an eye on this kettle, I'll be down in a few minutes."

She had had plenty of practice, there had been a great many abrupt departures during those twenty years. She packed the small black suitcase with brisk movements, and by the time she brought it down George had the tea made, and was shuffling papers together in his briefcase and locking his desk.

"Has the van driver seen a photograph of your man?" she asked, pouring tea.

"Yes, but he can't be too clear about anything but the general build and movements of the two he saw. It was night, and they had a powerful torch trained on him the moment he pulled up. We might get an identification when we can show him the man himself. But between you and me, I doubt it."

Bunty doubted it, too. The van-load of furs bound from the London dealer to Comerbourne's leading dress-shop had been hi-jacked shortly after leaving the motorway, on a night in early September, nearly six weeks past, and the driver was still in hospital. The wonder was that he had been able to tell them anything at all. A quiet stretch of road, a red triangle conspicuously displayed, a car askew, half off the road, a man running along the verge and waving a torch towards the cab of the big van—add up the details, and who wouldn't have deduced an accident, and stopped to help? The driver had seen a second man dart out of the shadow of the car, and he had an eye for the characteristics of movement, and insisted he would know this one again if he could ever see him in motion. But no sooner had he pulled in to the side of the road and jumped down from his cab than he was hit on the head from behind, by someone he never saw at all, and that was the last thing he knew about it. Hit three times, as it turned out, to make sure of him. He had a tough constitution and a hard skull, and he survived, and even remembered. But for him they would never have known where the attack took place, for the empty van was picked up later on a road-house parking-ground twenty miles off its route, and the driver was found in the morning dumped in the remotest corner of a lay-by on a country road in the opposite direction. Every part of the van that might have carried prints had been polished as clean as bone. A thoroughly professional job. And nobody had seen hide or hair of the load of furs since then. Probably they had been delivered to an already waiting customer that same night.

If Midshire had had any doubts, after that, that crime on a big-business scale was moving in on its territory, the wage-snatch three weeks later would have settled the matter. But the driver who regularly conveyed Armitage Pressings' weekly pay-roll to the factory on Thursdays had not provided any information for the police, because he had been unconscious when the ambulance-men lifted him on to the stretcher, and dead before they got him to hospital. As for the van, someone had ditched it among the skeletons in a local scrap-yard within an hour of the crime.

And this time the weapon they had used on him had not been a cosh, but a gun. Guns had seldom featured in Midshire crime before, and then usually in the haphazard and amateur kind. This was professionalism on a highly organised scale. The planners were extending their territory, and it looked as if the march of progress had reached Comer-bourne.

" I'd better get off," said George, sighing, and rose to pick up his case

" I'll come in with you." Bunty got up very quickly, and whisked out into the hall for her coat. " You can drop me off at the Betterbuy, and I'll get a bus back. I want to pick up a few things there."

There was nothing she needed, but with his preoccupations he couldn't hope to read that in her face, which was bright, tranquil and sensible as always. The truth was that she had suddenly felt her very bones ache at the thought of seeing him go, and being alone in the house with the autumnal chill and silence after he was gone. Even a few minutes was worth buying; even the struggle on to a crowded bus on the way back might break the spell of her isolation, and restore her to the company of her neighbours. Tiresome, troublous and abrasive as one's fellow-men can be, only the friction of human contact keeps one man-alive.

"I thought you hated the supermarket," said George obtusely, frowning over his own anxieties, and smiling through them abstractedly at his wife. He had loved her ever since he was twenty-two and she eighteen, and so whole-heartedly and firmly that talking to her was something as secret as confiding in his own conscience; which was why she seldom questioned him, and he never hesitated to tell her what troubled him. No betrayal was involved; it was a conversation with himself. Only occasionally, as now, did he stiffen suddenly to the devastating doubt whether she in return opened her own agonies to him, or whether there was something there denied to him for reasons which diminished him, and removed her to a distance he could not bear. The moments of doubt were appalling, pin-points of dismay, but unbelievably brief, vanished always before he could pursue them, and forgotten before they could undermine his certainty. But he never knew whether this was because they were delusions, inspired by some private devil, or whether she diagnosed them and herself plucked them out of his consciousness before they could sting. She was, after all, the antidote to all evils. How could he know whether the exorcism worked as efficiently the other way?

"I do hate the place," said Bunty warmly, "but what choice have I got? Haven't you noticed that all our four groceries in Comerford have switched over to self-service?"

"I thought it was supposed to make shopping quicker and easier," he said vaguely. What he was thinking was how beautiful she was, his forty-year-old wife, how much more beautiful now with her few silvery hairs among the thick chestnut waves, and the deep lines of character and laughter and rueful affection in her face, than the unblemished ivory girl of twenty years ago. Those smooth, eager, glowing young things are so touching, when you know only too well what's waiting for them. They don't all weather and mature into such splendour as this.

"Hah! You try it! Getting round is all right, once you

know where everything is, but getting out is the devil. Give me the old corner gossip-shop every time. You could hang around if you weren't holding anyone else up, and get out fast if you were. And no damned stamps!" said Bunty feelingly. "But that's progress for you— all part of the same process. We've all got to get mechanised, like the criminals."

They went out to the car together, the house darkened and locked behind them. Once in the car shoulder to shoulder, with the doors fast closed against the dull rain and the muddy remnant of the light, they recovered a certain security. The demons clawed at the glass impotently, tracing greasy runnels of water through devious channels down the panes, splitting the street lights into a dozen flat, refracted slivers of sulphur-yellow, smoky playing-cards shuffled in an invisible hand. The raw new bungalows on the other side of their own residential road perforated the darkness with eruptions of pink, featureless brick.

"Change and decay!" said Bunty bitterly. She hadn't meant to say it, it was all too plain. The population explosion must settle somewhere, but homes ought to have a certain reticence, as well as a degree of assurance, and these were hesitant, at once aggressive and apologetic, meant for units, not families.

"I know! You wouldn't think this was just a village when we settled here, would you? With about three service shops, and farms right on the through road, and a pet river like a tortoise-shell kitten chasing leaves all down the back-gardens."

"Careful!" said Bunty. "You're getting lyrical."

"I'm getting homesick. For the past. It's a sign of age creeping on. By any standards, this is a town now. You don't notice it sneaking in, but suddenly there it is. Chain shops, supermarkets, bingo halls and all. Automatic-barrier parking-grounds, gift stamps, special offers, fourpence off—the lot! Bunty, let's move!"

"It used to be so lovely," she said; and then, reasonably: " We couldn't go anywhere that it wouldn't catch up with us. Why run?"

In the main street, which had once been the road through the village, neon lights peered shortsightedly through the murk, all their greens and blues and reds filmed over with sour grey gloom. The jostling cars of the affluent society glared shoulder to shoulder from the new car parks, their colours dimmed with thin, glutinous mud. The cinema frontage sustained with evident effort an almost-nude blonde twelve feet long, sprawled the length of its lights, three feet of flaxen hair extending her at the head, as though someone had dragged her there by those pale ropes. She wore a bikini, and she might have been merely sun-bathing, but she looked dead. There was no queue to find out the truth; no one was interested.

" Wait till you see what they're doing with old Pearce's place," said George, between resignation and revulsion. " Or didn't I tell you he's sold out? To some chain moving in from the south. He had too good a spot to survive long, once the urbanisation started."

He turned the car left out of the High Street, and slowed as he approached the glittering frontage of what had once been Pearce's Garage, long inhabited by three generations of passionate motor-maniacs without a grain of commercial acumen between them, but able to do just about anything with an engine. All its capital had been in the background then, and the forecourt and petrol sales had been a somewhat tedious chore, very modestly lit and little regarded. No advertising was needed for a first-class service to which every well-run car in the county knew its own way.

Within ten days of the sale things had changed radically. A long festoon of lights in four colours stretched all along the frontage, which was being torn back into a great arc to accommodate nine new pumps of the latest type. They looked more like something from outer space than mere petrol pumps. A large neon sign over a repainted office flaunted the name of the chain in the single word: FLEET.

Two large posters in fluorescent orange proclaimed apocryphally: "Double stamps' week!"

"See?" said George, with bitter satisfaction.

"Oh, well," sighed Bunty helplessly. "He was pushing retiring age anyhow, and the offer must have been monumental."

"Still, if Tony hadn't emigrated his dad would never have sold out," observed George, drawing the Morris neatly into position by the nearest Super pump. He opened the door and slid out as a snub-nosed, shaggy-headed youngster came loping down from the office in answer to the bell. "Fill her up, Bobby."

"Sure, Mr. Felse!" The sombre young face brightened faintly at the sight of them. Bobby had been on probation, an apparently incurable driver-away of unlocked cars, when George had followed a hunch and talked old Pearce into taking him on and giving him a gloriously legitimate interest in the machines he couldn't resist. George found himself hoping that two years had been long enough to effect a cure, because he felt in his bones that this experiment wasn't going to survive the change of ownership. Commercial garage chains have very little interest in the salvation of local problem children. In such a county as Midshire, however, there are still plenty of family businesses in the remoter areas, and a two-year apprenticeship with Pearce's is a very sound recommendation.

"Well, how's it coming along?" said George, avoiding any appearance of actual concern.

"Not sure it is, Mr. Felse." Bobby frowned darkly over the purling petrol, watching the level with dubious eyes. "You know how it is, you get used to certain people's ways. I don't reckon this lot care all that much about cars." He delivered this indictment of blasphemy with more sorrow than anger.

"Then you'll be all the more likely to score a personal hit," said George reasonably, "since you do."

"Well, maybe—but they don't really want you to. It's

the quick money they're interested in. *You* know! Make it *look* good, and that's it. The money's out here, really, not back in the workshops. Not unless you can pick up a nice juicy insurance job," said Bobby disdainfully, and withdrew the pipe accurately and dexterously at the crucial moment. He hung it up, and wiped the neck of the tank, though it was spotless. " I don't reckon I shall be here long, Mr. Felse."

" What's the pinch?" asked George easily. " The new boss?"

Bobby shrugged and grinned. " *He* wouldn't matter so much, we shan't be seeing much of him, anyhow. Thirty-seven of these stations they say he's got now, most of 'em in London and the south. We're about the most northerly yet. No, *he* wouldn't matter. It's this new manager he's put in. Proper thruster he looks like being—you know, town style, all flash and everything on the surface." Bobby counted change expertly, with one eye on the new, large window of the office, festooned with pot plants. " That's him now, just coming out on the concrete—the one who looks like a bruiser."

Two men had emerged from the glass doorway, and were pacing the length of the concreted arc, studying the renovations with critical approval. The one in the white overall was large-chested and thick of feature, and had a peeled-down, aggressive confidence in his manner that would not have been out of place in either a boxing ring or a sales ring. The other was several inches taller, a long-striding, elegant figure in a pearl-grey suit.

" *Mister* Mostyn," said Bobby, eyeing the distant white figure with eloquent dislike. " Don't you never let him sell you a used car, Mr. Felse, that's all!"

" Who's the other?" asked George, pocketing his change.

" Oh, that's the boss . . . that's Fleet himself. Been looking his buy over and viewing the development plans. Mostyn had me working on *his* car this afternoon . . . believe me, that was *one* he wanted done properly." He

closed the door firmly upon George, and waved a hand.
"See you, Mr. Felse!"

"So long, Bobby! Just give it a whirl before you make
up your mind. But he'll go," George prophesied the next
moment, for Bunty's ear alone. "That's not his kind of
set-up now."

The Morris wheeled back from the apron on to a dark,
slimily gleaming street, and the long festoons of lights
slithered away behind them. They re-entered the main
street at the next corner, close to the southern edge of the
town now, with the ordered glimmer of the new housing
estate of Well Meadow terraced up the green slope in the
darkness ahead. Across the street the six plate-glass
windows of the Betterbuy supermarket glared steamily,
plastered with bargain offers in poison green and electric
orange.

"Not my kind, either," Bunty sighed, and reached over
into the back seat for her basket and handbag, as the car
hissed to a standstill in the thin ooze alongside the kerb.
"But if you'll believe me, this is the only place in Comerford where I can buy whole black pepper!"

At this last moment it felt like tearing herself in two
to get out of the car and leave him behind, but a kerbside
stop affords no time for hesitation. She cast the usual
quick glance behind, opened the door of the Morris, and
slid her feet out to the greasy pavement, tilting her cheek
back at the same moment for George's customary kiss.

"Good luck, then, mate! I'll expect you when I see
you."

"Just as soon as I can make it. 'Bye, darling, take care
of yourself."

"Listen who's talking," said Bunty derisively. "*I'm*
not the one who goes hobnobbing with gunmen and such."

She was on her feet in a light leap, the door slammed,
the car gathered way and was gone, its rear lights dwind-
ling to cigarette-ends just visible in the soiled, wet darkness,
as it rounded the curve by the White Hart. And that,

thought Bunty, is how it should be done, when it has to be done at all. She furled in the frayed cords of her personality that had been torn loose with George's departure, but this time the ache did not dull, and the bleeding did not stop.

Any one of those separations in the past twenty years might have been the final one; even before the armed professionals arrived on the scene, a policeman's hadn't been the safest of careers. Is it only on the edge of middle age, she wondered, that you begin admitting the possibility? Or, more simply, do you never even notice it until then?

Overheated air closed round her like warm treacle as she pushed her way into the supermarket, and made for the dry goods' shelves. Even husbands who take their cars out in the morning to drive tranquilly to work in banks and shops may be heading unawares for a pile-up at the first corner, or a hold-up and a shot over the counter. But life would be impossible if their wives spent every separated moment thinking so.

::   ::

She sat in the empty, silent house, brushing her hair before the glass and watching her mirrored face as if the secret of this unforeseen and inescapable dismay lay there behind her own eyes. She had avoided the bus, after all, and walked all the way home through the thin, unclean rain, in the dim, amorphous colourings of evening and autumn, inexpressibly elegiac and sad. And where there should have been shelter, under her own roof, the other darkness had closed down appallingly on her spirit, the darkness you see when you look over your shoulder half-way through life.

How was it that she had turned forty without a chilling thought, and now at forty-one must run head-on into the skeleton in the way?

It happens to everyone, sooner or later, even the best balanced and happiest, that sudden hesitation and the long first look behind, the first qualm of wondering whether

all has been well done, whether there is really anything
there at all to record the course of a life suddenly seen to be
half-over. October is a searching time even for the young,
but for them it is only a seasonal disquiet, they have the
renewal of Spring within them, they have good cause to
believe in it. Bunty's heart ached inconsolably for the
beauty that was gone, for the youth that would not renew
itself. She looked into her own eyes, and they were no
longer unaware of passing time, and no longer innocent of
the implications, age, infirmity and death.

She had turned out the main light in the room. Her
brush crackled and sparkled through her thick brown hair
in the dimness, and her eyes stared back at her unwaver-
ingly from the glass, sometimes obscured by the swaying
strands of hair, but always constant and naked in their
questioning when the curtain parted again. What is the
matter with you? she asked the image that fronted her.
They were two, not one, there might even be an answer.
You're a lucky woman, a happy woman. You've always
been aware of it. You have a husband you love, and a son
you adore, you are equable and outgoing by temperament;
in a modest way, which has always satisfied you up to now,
you have every possible blessing. Even a sense of humour!
Or have you? Or has it only been mislaid for a short test-
ing time?

And that's all? wondered the eyes confronting her. And
that's enough?

The clouds were breaking outside the window, but only
in tormented shapes of scudding flight and bitter pursuit,
driven by a sudden wailing wind. All the too static air was
abruptly in motion. She felt time rushing away from
under her feet, leaving her falling through space in a howling greyness. There had once been a certain Bunty Elliott
who had known beyond question that she was going to be a
great singer, and leave a treasury of recorded music that
would make her immortal. But she had never put her gifts
to any serious test, because she had met and married George

Felse, and turned into a mere wife, a policeman's wife. And what was she now but George's wife—no, George's grass widow at this moment, and this moment was her whole life in microcosm—and Dominic's mother? Did she exist, except as a reflection of them? Was she condemned only to act, only to be anything at all through her husband and her son?

What had become of Bunty herself? Somewhere she had got lost between George and Dominic, and rediscovery would not be easy. George's face looked up at her from the photograph on her dressing-table, ten years younger than now but essentially the same, grave, thin, thoughtful, with dark, steady eyes, and sensitive lines about his mouth. She could paint in for herself the new furrows that had grown deep into his flesh since the picture was taken, and they added to his worth and significance, which were not and never would be in question. She loved him so naturally that she had never had cause to stop and assess how much she loved him. He, nevertheless, had an identity of his own, and was in no danger of losing it. And she?

If you were here now, she thought, you would be enough to restore the balance; I should be over the crest and on my way home. Why aren't you here? Why did you have to be somewhere else on this night of all nights?

And her son? Dominic was complicated, fascinating and absorbing, because he was half George and half herself. They had been devoted friends all his short life. She could even laugh at him, and not be excommunicated. But they grow up, and grow away. Dominic was at Oxford, with exams hanging over him, and Dominic had chosen a girl, and chosen her for life, for better or worse, for richer or poorer, for all time and with all his heart. Maybe he himself didn't yet know it, maybe he was too close to Tossa Barber to take in her full significance. But Bunty knew it. And approved it. He might have made so many mistakes, but in the event his instinct was true enough, and his choice sharp and sure. And she was glad. But where, now, was Bunty?

She had been prepared, insofar as any woman can be prepared, to be sloughed like an outworn skin. It presented no problem in her relationship with him, or even with his Tossa. But she was confronting the shell of Bunty Felse, and coming to terms with that gutted presence was not so easy.

What am I now? she thought. Am I anything? Yes, to George, certainly. I have a reason for going on being, I have a hollow to fill, maybe a bigger hollow than before. But whether I have enough substance to supply the vacuum, that's another matter. And whether anything exists which is truly me, and not reflections of these two, God only knows!

The bed was smooth, sterile and cold. She lay in the panting, unquiet darkness, and did not sleep. And in the morning, which was her forty-first birthday, there was no letter from Dominic and no telephone call from George. The early light of Saturday was grey, chill and calm, and she was utterly alone for perhaps the first time in her life. In a life which was half over, and shrinking in upon her even as she dressed to face it.

CHAPTER II

SHE COULD HAVE called up her friends, of course; she had plenty of friends. But with them she would simply have worn her normal face and manner, and kept her own counsel. You do not burden your friends with a sudden stranger half-way to the grave. You hide yourself while the darkness lasts—being, even at this crisis, reasonably secure that it will not last long—and emerge when you are yourself as they know you, and fit for their society again. No,

at this moment what you need is a stranger in an express
train, someone you need never see again, one of those
accidental priests in the fleeting confessionals of this life
where souls are often saved against the odds.

That was why she took herself for a long, solitary walk
that Saturday evening in October, avoiding the places most
familiar to her, and the haunts where her friends might
be. The air was dove-coloured and still since noon, chilling by dusk to the edge of frost, but never quite touching
it. The cloud was low and grey, but the atmosphere beneath it was clear. If it froze by morning, the crests of the
roads, at least, would dry, and the film of slime would
corrode away in pale dust.

The silence at home had helped to drive her out, but the
silence here on the country roads two miles from Comerford was vaster and even more oppressive. She had never
been afraid to walk alone in the night, not here; in a city
she might have been warier. She met shadows, and, occasionally responsive to some alchemy of recognition in anony-
mity, exchanged good nights with shadows. She kept aloof
from the roads that carried traffic, and the few cars she met
passed mysteriously, absorbed in their own missions. And
where she came at length to the main road again, she found
herself before the broad car park and polished frontage of
a modern roadhouse, the sort of place where none of her
acquaintance could possibly be encountered.

"The Constellation Orion"; a beautifully imaginative
name, at least. She remembered the place being opened,
though she had never been inside it. Well, why not now?
The building, twentieth-century metal box crossed with
by-pass Georgian, didn't live up to its name, but surely
promised strangers as transitory as any to be met with in
express trains. And she had plenty of time to walk home, all
night if need be; she had nobody at home waiting for her.

Warmth and noise met her in the doorway. The saloon
bar was so aggressively modern that it had almost reverted
to the jazz-age angularity of the twenties, and its décor

reminded her of fair-ground vases from her childhood. It was almost uncomfortably full. For some reason the same degree of actual discomfort in the bar itself seemed more acceptable. The lighting was mellower and milder there, and it was clearly the only room the locals, if they used this place at all, would dream of frequenting. Bunty edged her way to the bar-counter, bought herself a modest half of bitter, and carried it to a remote corner where a young couple had just vacated two chairs at a spindly table. Over the rim of her glass she surveyed the company, and let the confused roar of their many conversations drum in her ears without any effort to disentangle words. There was no one whom she knew, and no one who knew her. Nobody was interested, either; in twos, in threes, in shifting groups, they pursued their own preoccupations, and left her to hers.

She had been sitting there in her corner for ten minutes or so before she noticed the only other person who seemed to be alone. She saw him first over the shoulders of two sporty types in mohair car coats, and from his position he might easily have been a part of their circle; but emphatically his face denied it. He looked at them out of another world, a world as private and closed as hers. Quite a young man, maybe somewhere in his late twenties, maybe even turned thirty. Tall, a light-weight but well enough made, rather brittle and nervous in his movements, his straight dark hair disordered. What she noticed first was the greyish pallor of his face, and its tight stillness, like a clay mask, so apparently rigid that the sudden nervous quiver of one cheek was shocking, as though the whole face might be shattered. The taut surfaces quaked and recomposed themselves into the same stony tension. Deep within this defensive earthwork dark eyes, alert and bright to fever-point, kept watch from ambush, glaring from bruised, blue-rimmed sockets. He looked as if he had been on the tiles for two or three nights in succession; but she noted that the hand that held his glass was large, capable and perfectly steady.

He was getting too tightly hemmed in by the group at the bar. She saw him heave himself clear of them, edge back into the open, and look round for a more peaceful place. His ranging glance lit upon the single chair still vacant in her corner, and he started towards it.

Then he saw her. Really saw her, not as any unknown woman sitting there, but as this one particular woman, taken in entire in one flash of genuine concentration. It was the first time he had been fully aware of anyone in that room except himself and the personal devil with which he was surely at grips. He halted for a moment, poised quite still in the middle of the shifting, chattering, smoky bar, his eyes fixed on her. She thought that he almost drew back and turned away, that if she had lowered her eyes or looked through him he would have done it; but she looked back at him steadily and thoughtfully, neither inviting nor repulsing him, unless it was an invitation to show interest in him at all. One person under stress recognises another.

The moment of hesitation was gone; he came on with a quickened step. He had a whisky glass in one hand and a small bottle of ginger ale in the other. A long little finger touched tentatively at the back of the vacant chair.

"Do you mind if I sit here?" The voice was low-pitched but abrupt, as though he had to measure it out with care and constraint.

"Of course not, help yourself!"

She moved her glass to make room for his on the tiny table. It had a tray top of beaten brass that had never been nearer Benares than Birmingham. He looked at it for the fraction of an instant with disbelief, and then sat down carefully, and looked up at her.

"I agree," said Bunty with detachment. "It's rather nasty, but it's somewhere to put things down."

Something kindled in his face, no more than a momentary easing and warming of the haggard lines of his mouth, and a brisk spark that was burned out instantly in the intensity of his eyes.

"You didn't *look* as if you belonged here," he said. "Why *are* you here?"

Conversation came out of him without premeditation, and indeed with a famished urgency that ruled out premeditation, but in brief, jerky sentences, spurting from the muted violence that filled him. Violence was the word that first occurred to her, but she found it unacceptable on reflection; agitation might have been nearer the mark, or simply excitement. There was nothing impertinent in his manner, and whatever he was looking for, it wasn't a pick-up.

"Because I was alone," she said, with a directness equal to his own. "Why are you?"

"The same reason, I suppose. And I needed a drink."

It appeared that this was no more than the truth. The whisky had brought a faint warmth of colour into his clay mask, its frozen lines were at least growing pliable now.

"You don't mind my talking to you? I'll shut up if you say so."

She did not say so. What she did say, after a moment of deliberation, was: "I came out because it was too silent at home, and I came in here because it was even more silent outside."

He uttered a short, harsh sound that might, if he had been less tense, have emerged as a laugh. "That won't be our trouble here, anyhow. Or would you say this was a kind of silence, too? A howling silence?" The babel was reaching its climax, it was only half an hour to closing-time. The young man cast one brief glance round the room, and turned back to her, his eyes for a moment wide and dark with awareness of her, and strangely innocent of curiosity. "We've got something in common, then," he said, emptying his glass without taking his eyes from Bunty's face. "You weren't expecting to be alone, either."

"No," she agreed, thinking how different a celebration this forty-first birthday might have been, "I wasn't expecting to be alone."

"Nor was I. I'm heading north," he said jerkily, re-volving the empty glass dangerously between his fingers, "for a long week-end. Not much to look forward to now, though. There should have been two of us, if everything hadn't come to pieces." The glass was suddenly still be-tween his long hands; he stared at it blackly. "I suppose I ought to lay off, but I've got to have one more of these, I'm still twenty per cent short of human. May I get you the other half? Or would you prefer a short?"

"Thanks, the other half would be fine."

She watched him worm his way to the bar with the empty glasses, and knew that she had done that deliber-ately. Why? Because if she had refused he would have taken it as a rebuff and been turned in again upon his own arid company? Or because she would have lost touch with him and been driven back upon hers? What she was courting was the loss of herself in another human creature, and that was what he wanted, too. Not that it would ever be much more than two parallel monologues, the passing of two trains on a double track, somewhere in the dark. But at least the sight of a human face at one of the flying windows would assure the watcher of companionship in his wakefulness. Their need was mutual, why pass up the opportunity of filling it?

So she waited for him, and watched him come back to her, balancing full glasses carefully as he wound his way between the jostling backs of the Saturday-night crowd.

"I'm sorry about your spoiled week-end," she said. And with carefully measured detachment, since clearly this was no light matter to him at the moment: "Of course, there *are* other girls."

He was just setting down his glass on the table, and for the first time his hand shook. She looked up in surprise, and met his eyes at close range, suddenly fallen blank in a frozen face, as grey and opaque as unlighted glass. He sat down slowly, every line of his body drawn so taut that the air between them quivered.

" *Who mentioned a girl?*"

"There are only two sorts," she said patiently. "There was at least a fifty-fifty chance of guessing right first time about the companion who let you down."

He drew in a long, cautious breath and relaxed a little. The slow fires came back distrustfully into his eyes. " Yes ... I suppose it wasn't difficult." His voice groped through the words syllable by syllable, like feet in the dark feeling their way. "We fell out," he said. " It's finished. I can't say I wasn't warned, at least half a dozen of my friends must have told me she was playing me for a sucker, but I never believed it."

"You could still be right about her," said Bunty reasonably, " and they could still be wrong."

"Not a chance! It all blew up in my face to-day. For good."

"There may be more to be said for her than you think now. You may not always feel like this. You and she may make it up again, given a little goodwill."

" No!" he said with quiet violence. " That's out! She'll never have the chance to let me down again."

"Then—at the risk of repeating myself—there *are* other girls."

He wasn't listening. No doubt he heard the sound of her voice quite clearly, just as those blue-circled, burning eyes of his were memorising her face, but all he saw and all he heard had to do with his own private pain. Bunty was merely a vessel set to receive the overflow of his distress.

"We only got engaged ten days ago," he said. " God knows why she ever said yes, she had this other fellow on the string all along. Whatever she wanted out of it, it wasn't me."

" It happens," said Bunty. " When you commit yourself to another person you take that risk. There isn't any way of hedging your bet."

" She hedged hers pretty successfully," he said bitterly.

"She wasn't committed. And you're better off without her."

So softly that she hardly heard him, more to himself than to her, he said, "Oh, my God, what is there in it, either way?" His hands clenched into white-knuckled fists on his knees. She thought for a moment that he was going to faint, and instinctively put out a hand and took him by the arm, no hesitant touch, but a firm grip, tethering him fast to the world it seemed he would gladly have shaken off in favour of darkness. It brought his head up with a jerk, his eyes dazed and dark in that blanched face. They stared steadily at each other for a moment, devouring line and substance and form so intensely that neither of them would ever be able to hide from the other again, under any name or in any disguise.

"Look," said Bunty quietly, "you're not fit to drive any distance to-night. Go home, fall into bed, sleep her off, drink her off if you have to, get another girl, anything, only give yourself a chance. It isn't the end of the world . . . it had damned well better not be! You've got a life before you, and it isn't owed to her, it's owed in part to the rest of us, but mostly to yourself. You go under and we've all lost."

She wondered if he even knew that she was at least twelve years older than he was. She had begun by feeling something like twenty years older, and now she was no longer sure that there was even a year between them. This was no adolescent agony, but a mature passion that shook the whole room, even though the babel went on round it, oblivious and superficial, a backcloth of triviality.

"It *is* the end of the world," said the young man, quite softly and simply. "That's what you don't understand."

The clock behind the bar began to chime with an unexpected, silvery sound.

"Time!" called the barman, pitching his voice on the same mellifluous note. "Time, gentlemen, please!"

: :   : :

She spent an unnecessary few minutes in the cloakroom, tidying her hair and repairing her lipstick, not so much to escape from him as to give him every chance to escape from her if he wanted to. Men are much more likely than women to repent of having said too much and stripped themselves too naked, and it might well be that now, having unloaded the worst of his burden, he would prefer to make off into the darkness and never see or think of her again. But when she stepped out from the lighted doorway, under the silver stars of the sign, he was there waiting for her, a slender, tense shadow beside the low chain fence of the car park. She felt no surprise and no uneasiness.

"Have you got transport? Then may I give you a lift home?"

"It's out of your way," she said equably. "I live in Comerford, and I imagine you're heading for the M.6."

"It won't add more than three miles to the distance. And there's nobody waiting for me," he said tightly. She was growing used to that tone, but it still puzzled her, because for all its muted desperation it was strangely innocent of self-pity.

"Then if you don't mind going round that way, I should be glad to ride with you." Why not? All he wanted was to warm his hands at this tiny fire for a few minutes longer. And she could take care of herself. She was a mature woman, self-reliant and well-balanced, she was not afraid to venture nearer to another person, not afraid that she would not be able to control the relationship, even extricate herself from it if the need arose. She was old enough to be able to offer him the companionship he needed, and not have it mistaken for something else.

His hand touched her arm punctiliously as they walked across to the car, but he kept the touch light and tentative, as if mortally afraid of damaging the grain of comfort he had got out of her. The broad space of tarmac was emptying fast, the last few cars peeling off in turn between

the white posts of the exit. Soon they would have the night
to themselves on the dark country road into Comerford.

" Here we are ! "

He leaned to open the door for her, and closed it upon
her as soon as she was settled. She was incorrigibly ignor-
ant about cars, and worse, in the view of her family, she
was completely incurious. Cars were a convenient means of
getting from here to there, and sometimes they were
beautiful in themselves, but they made no other impression
upon her. This one was large but not new, and by no
means showy, short on chrome but long on power under
the bonnet, and he handled it as though he knew what to
do with all the power he could get, and probably consider-
ably more than he could afford. Bunty might have no
mechanical sense at all, but she had an instinctive appreciation of competence.

" Have you very far to go?" she asked, watching the
drawn profile beside her appearing and disappearing fit-
fully as they passed the last lights of the frontage and took
the Comerford road.

" About three hundred miles. It won't take me long.
It's a quicker run by night."

" Maybe . . . but all the same I wish you'd go home to
bed. I don't feel happy about you setting off on a run
like that, in the state you're in."

" There's nothing the matter with my state. I'm not
drunk," he said defensively.

" I know you're not. I didn't mean that. But in any
case, it isn't going to be a very long week-end, is it, to be
worth such a journey? It's nearly Sunday already. And
you did say there was no one waiting for you." The silence
beside her ached, but was not inimical. " Am I trespass-
ing?" she asked simply.

" No!" It was the first time she had heard warmth in his
voice. " You're very kind. But I've got to go. I can't
stay here now. It won't be such a short stay as all that,

you see, I'm not due back till Wednesday. Don't worry about me, I shall be all right."

Abruptly she asked: "When did you last eat?"

Astonished, he peered back into the recesses of his memory, and admitted blankly: "I don't even know! Yes, wait . . . I did have a lunch . . . of sorts, anyhow. Opened a tin . . . one of those repulsive dinky grills."

"Nothing since then?"

"No . . . I suppose not! I haven't wanted anything."

"No wonder you look sick," she said practically. "You'd be wanting something before you got to the end of your journey, believe me. And those two whiskys will settle better with some food inside you. If Lennie hasn't closed up his stall we'll stop there and pick up some sandwiches or hot dogs for you, and a coffee."

"I suppose," he admitted, "it might be an idea."

The lights of Comerford winked ahead of them, orange stars against a moist black sky. Old Lennie's coffee-stall always spent Saturday evening on the narrow forecourt before the old market cross, handy for the late crowds emerging from the Bingo hall and the billiard club. All the new estates and the commercial development lay at the other end of the town, and this approach across the little river might still have been leading them into the old, sprawling village the place had once been. A foursquare Baptist chapel, built a hundred years ago of pale grey brick, looked out across the water between pollarded trees. Once over the slight hump of the bridge, they could see the white van of the coffee-stall gilded by the street lamp above it, and with its own interior light still burning. The small, lame proprietor, hurt in a pit accident twenty-five years ago, was just clearing his counter.

"Pull in for a minute and drop me," ordered Bunty, "and I'll see what he's got left. We can't park here, but we can turn down by the riverside and find a place there for you to eat in peace."

She was back in a minute or two with two paper bags and a waxed carton of coffee.

" It's a good thing Lennie knows me so well, he wouldn't have opened up again for everybody, not after he's cashed up."

The old man had come limping out from his stall to close the shutter, and stood looking after his customer now with candid curiosity, watching her tuck her long legs into a strange car, beside a strange young man. He stood stolidly gazing, with no pretence at other preoccupations, as the car took the right-hand turn that would bring it down towards the park and the riverside gardens.

" This is all right, anywhere here. This is only a loop road, it brings us back to the main one just before the lights. We shan't be in anyone's way here, there won't be much traffic at this time of night."

There were no houses along here, and hence no homeless cars parked overnight outside them, an inevitable phenomenon in every urbanisation. He halted the car with its hub-caps brushing the overgrown grass under the trees. A narrow path and a box hedge separated them from the park on this near side, and across the road, beyond fifty yards of ornamental shrubbery and trees, the Comer gleamed faintly. After he had stopped the engine it was very quiet, and unaccountably still, as if every necessity for measuring time had stopped. Nobody was waiting for either of them at the end of their journey.

Suddenly she felt him shaking beside her, the only shaken thing in all that stillness. It happened as soon as he took his hands from the wheel and let his concentration relax, and for a full minute of struggle he could not suppress the shudders that pulsed through him. Bunty tore open the waxed carton of coffee and put it into his hand, closing her own fingers over his to guide the cup to his lips. He drank submissively, and presently drew a long, cautious breath, and let it out again in a great, relaxing sigh, and she felt his tensed flesh soften again into ease.

"I'm sorry . . . I'm all right, just more tired than I realised."

"At least get some food inside you and rest for a bit." She dumped the paper bags of sausage rolls and ham sandwiches on his knees, and watched him eat, at first with weary obedience and little interest, then with sudden astonished greed, as though he had just discovered food. "You see, you were hungry." She sat nursing the half-empty coffee carton, studying the shadowy form beside her with a frown.

"Look, you simply can't go on with this, it would be crazy."

"Maybe I am crazy," he said perversely. "Did you ever think of that? You were right about the food, though. Look, I owe you for all this, you must let me . . ."

"My round," said Bunty. "A return for the other half."

He didn't argue. He stretched himself with a huge sigh that racked and then released him from head to foot, and lay back in the driving seat, turning his forehead to rest against the glass. A large hand crumpled the empty paper bags and held them loosely on his knee.

"Better?"

"Much better!"

"Then listen! You shouldn't go on to-night. It isn't fair to other road-users to drive when you're as exhausted as this. You might pass out on the motorway, what then?"

"I shan't pass out on the motorway," he said through a shivering yawn, "I can't afford to." The note of grim certainty sank into a mumble; he yawned again. "No choice," he said distantly, "no choice at all. . . ."

She sat silent for a while, though she had had much more to urge upon him; for after all, she told herself, he was not hers. And the moment that thought was formulated she knew that he was, that he had been hers since the moment she had accepted him. Now she didn't know what to do about him. People to whom you have once opened your doors can't afterwards be thrown out, but neither can they be kept against their will. If he would go on, he would, and she had no right to prevent him even if she could. Only then did it occur to her how completely, during this last hour and a half, she had forgotten about herself.

What drew her out of her brooding speculation was the rhythm of his breathing, long and easy and regular, misting the glass against his cheek. He was asleep. The hand that lay open on his knee still cradled the crumpled paper-bags; she lifted them delicately out of his hold and dropped them into the empty carton, and he never moved.

So it seemed that she had nothing left to do here, after all. She didn't even consider waking him; sleep was probably the thing he most needed, and perhaps if he had his rest out he would wake up ready to see sense and go home. And you, she told herself, might just as well do the same. It was no distance from here, she could walk it in ten minutes. A pity, in a way, to slip away without a good-bye, but these encounters are sometimes better ended without ceremony, and the partners in them don't need any formulæ in order to understand and remember them.

She waited a little while, but he was deeply asleep, she could easily depart without disturbing him. The sky had cleared overhead, there were stars, and the moisture in the air would be rime by morning. Not a good night to be sleeping out in a car. Maybe he had a rug tucked away somewhere, old cars without modern heaters often carry them as a matter of course. She looked round on the back seat, but there was nothing there but his suitcase. If there was a rug that lived permanently in the car, it might be in the boot; and there were his keys, dangling in the ignition close to her hand. Would he regard it as a breach of their delicate, unformulated agreement if she made use of them to look for something to cover him?

She hesitated for a few moments over that question, but when it came to the point she knew she could not leave him to wake up half-frozen in a rimy dawn. She raised her hand to the keys, and carefully drew them out, and her companion slept on peacefully. Quietly she opened the door, and quietly closed it after her.

The black butt-end of the car was as broad as a cab. There was enough light for her to find the lock easily, and the key was the second she tried. The large lid of the boot gave with a faint creak, and lifted readily. Faint starlight spilled over the rim into the dark interior, but called into being only vague shapes under the shadow of the lid. She felt forward into the dimness, and her hand found something woolly and soft, but with a hard stiffness inside it that rocked gently to her touch. She felt her way along it, and her fingers slipped from its edge and grasped something cold, articulated and rigid.

For one instant she was still, not recognising what she held; then she snatched back her hand with a hissing intake of breath, so sharply that the chill thing she touched was plucked momentarily towards her. With minute, terrible sounds the folded shapes within the boot shifted and rocked, leaning towards the open air as if they would rise and climb out to confront her. The marble hand she had grasped hung poised at the end of its sleeve. Something pale and silken and fine swung forward and flowed over Bunty's hand, encircling her frozen fingers in the curled ends of long, straight blonde hair.

The girl coiled up between the tool-box and the spare wheel was dead and stiffening. Until that blind touch disturbed her, she must have been lying like a child asleep. Her dark coat was unbuttoned over a cream-coloured sweater, and in the breast of the sweater, even by this curious, lambent half-light, a small round dot of darkness could be seen, crusted and rough-edged like a seal, the only indication of the manner in which she had died.

Bunty crouched, staring, her hands at her mouth, numbed and cold with shock.

So this was why that girl of his was never going to have the chance to let him down again, this was why he had to get out of here to-night at all costs. This was how their quarrel had ended.

CHAPTER III

A HAND REACHED past her shoulder and slammed the boot shut. And if there had ever been a moment when she could have turned and run, with a hope of eluding pursuit in the trees, it was already over, had passed unrecognised while she stood there incapable of utterance or movement, all her senses stunned with horror.

She had heard nothing, had seen nothing but the slight, contorted body before her; but something had roused him, the cold air as the car door opened, the cautious sound of the latch closing again, maybe even some subconscious instinct of self-preservation that needed no help from the physical senses. For there he was at her back, recoiling now to evade her touch, in case shock gave her the reckless courage to attempt any move against him, edging silently along the side of the car to show to her, and hide from anyone else who might choose this of all moments to come by, the small black gun levelled at her heart. His hand was still steady. And the evidence was there between them, hidden now but unforgettably present, that the gun was loaded, and that he knew how to use it.

"Keep quiet," he said, in a thread of a voice that had the tension of hysteria. "If you make a sound or a move, I shall kill you."

She was deathly quiet, and frenziedly still. Numbness clogged all her senses, but somewhere within her burned a core of intelligence frantically alert to all the possibilities, and quick to guard itself from any mistakes.

"My God, my God," he said in a howling whisper, to

himself rather than to her, "why did you? . . . *why did you?*"

Yes, why, she thought, her mind lost in this drugged body, groping like a sleepwalker, why did I? Because I felt responsible for you! See what it gets you, feeling responsible! This is involvement gone too far. But there wasn't any turning back; none for him, and none for her. She said nothing. As yet she had no voice, she couldn't have screamed for help even if the round black muzzle of the gun hadn't been trained on her with its one hypnotic eye. Screaming is, in any case, harder than you might suppose. It takes an experience of this kind to teach you how tough a resistance your sensible flesh, mind and spirit put up to believing in danger and death. Such things happen at a dream-distance, to others; never to you. When they do crop up in your way, like some skeleton apparition in a medieval legend, you don't believe in them. Not until you've had time to acclimatise. By which time it is too late to take avoiding action.

But this was reality. She wasn't at home in bed, dreaming it. There he was, in the soft, diffused light, rigid and quivering, but a hundred per cent awake and alert and dangerous, staring at her with bruised eyes now wide-open and impersonal as fate in a shadowless, porcelain face, over the gun which had become a third—no, a fourth—character in this impossible scene.

She looked down at the closed lid of the boot, and there was a tress of pale hair glimmering over the rim.

"Lock it," he said. And when she stooped mechanically to turn the key: "No . . . that hair . . . push it out of sight, all of it. . . ." The voice was thin, harsh and piercing, like broken glass.

She fumbled at the silvery tendrils, which seemed still to have such innocent, sparkling life in them. She tucked the last strand out of sight, and her fingertips touched the cold, ice-cold face. The chill passed out of the dead flesh into the living without revulsion; all she felt was a dreadful, quick-

ening pity over so much waste. She let down the lid gently,
like the lid of a coffin, and turned the key upon the body.
Slowly she straightened up and looked round blindly at the
man with the gun, the bunch of keys outstretched in her
hand.

" Put them on the wing between us," he said, and drew
back a step out of her reach, with infinite care to be silent
and restrained even in this movement. He didn't want to
startle her into some panicky reaction that would make the
shot necessary.

She laid down the keys where he indicated, releasing
them softly, with the same exaggerated caution against any
sound. And he reached out his free hand without taking
his eyes from her, and gathered them up and pocketed them.

" Let's have it clear." His voice was more assured now,
and deader, if there are degrees in death. " If you make a
single false move, even by mistake, I'll kill you. What
choice have you left me? You see I've nothing to lose now."

Her mind was beginning to work, clearly enough, but
like the logical threading of a dream. She saw, and acted in
accordance with what she saw. He had indeed nothing to
lose. His back was against a wall, and he was proof against
fears and scruples; and she was not going to make any
false move. She looked back at him, motionless and attentive, and said nothing.

" Get back in the car. I shall be close behind you."

She turned stiffly, obeying the motion of the hand that
held the gun, and slowly circled the back of the car and
walked to the passenger door. Slowly, in case he suspected her of an attempt at escape. She might, indeed,
have risked it if the car had been drawn up on the other
side of the road, but here there was only the narrow path
and then the thick hedge, nowhere at all for her to take
cover. He followed her step for step, she could feel the
muzzle of the gun not six inches from her back. The
transit of those four or five yards seemed to last a life-
time; at least it gave her a sudden dazzlingly clear distant

view of her own situation. Only a few hours ago she had
been laboriously extending her powers to cope with the
realisation that half her life had slipped away almost un-
noticed, and now she saw the other half bridged in one
monstrous leap, and death within touch of her hand.

No car came along. No one walked home by this way.
No belated lovers dawdled in the dark. In summer there
might have been a hope, there was none now. She was
on her own, and there was nothing she could possibly do
except obey him. Except, perhaps, leave some sign here
to be found?

Her handbag was on her wrist, and there was no chance
of opening it without being detected. But her purse was
in her left-hand coat pocket, and it contained a perspex
window in the flap, with her name and address in it.
Good-bye to seven pounds and some loose change, but
what did she need with money now? At least it would
show where she had been. She drew it out carefully but
quickly, the swinging handbag hiding the movements of
her hand, and tossed it slightly aside into the overgrown
autumnal grass that separated the footpath from the road.
It fell with very little sound, but she risked letting her
foot slip from the edge of the kerb in a noisy stumble to
cover the moment, and spread her right hand against the
car to steady herself. The man behind her drew in his
breath with a hiss of warning, alarm and pain, and the
muzzle of the gun prodded her back and sent an icy chill
down the marrow of her spine.

" *Be careful!*"

But he meant the stumble, not the purse she had thrown
away. All his attention was focused on her, he didn't
look aside into the grass. And now it was up to fate. If an
honest person found what she had left behind, he would
try to return it, and failing to find her at the address
given, take it to the police, who would most surely wonder
at her absence. If a dishonest person—or even a humanly
fallible one—found it . . . well, so much the worse.

He stepped past her at the appropriate moment, and held the door open for her. As soon as she was inside he slammed the door upon her and darted round to the driver's door; and as soon as he took his hand from her own door, she reached for it again, wrenched at the handle and flung her weight against it in a sudden passion of realisation that it was now or never. Leap out and run for it, back towards the cross. . . . The car's bulk would cover her for the first few moments, he would have to take aim afresh and in a hurry, she might get clean away.

The door held fast, the handle moved only part-way, and the thrust of her body was spent vainly. There was a safety catch with which she wasn't familiar, and she hadn't seen him set it before he slammed the door. By the time she had found it and was clawing at it frantically, he was in the driving seat beside her, and the car was in motion.

The door catch gave, the safety catch held. He reached a long arm across her and slammed the door to again, and she had lost her only chance, if it had ever been a chance. The impetus of their take-off flung her back in the seat, hard against his shoulder. The trees hissed by on either side at speed. To attempt to jump out now would be as good a way as any of committing suicide.

She sat with her hands clenched together in her lap, confronting the truth fully for the first time, and so closely that she saw nothing else. What difference could it possibly make who found her purse, or whether it was ever found at all, or how many police they turned out to look for her to-morrow? Nobody could get to her in time to be of any use; she was absolutely on her own, and her time must be short.

What could this man do now, except get rid of the witness?

: :   : :

He took the turn into the main street fast and expertly, and at such an angle that her mind, working with frosty clarity somewhere within the shell of shock, registered the certainty that he knew this town very well. Then she remembered the traffic lights. There was no way of evading that crossing in the middle of Comerford; and she knew, if he did not, that on Saturday nights there was usually a police constable keeping an eye unobtrusively on affairs there, at least until all the Espresso bar and motorbike brigade had gone home to bed, which they seldom did until after midnight. Now if the lights should be against them there . . .

There were still several groups of young people conducting their leisurely and noisy farewells along the pavement when the car drew near to the crossroads. The dance at the Regal wasn't over yet, and there was P.C. Peter Hillard standing by the window of the jeweller's shop looking at nothing and watching everything, with his hands linked behind him, and the usual deceptive expression of benign idiocy on his face. Now if the lights were at red, surely she dared. . . . He wouldn't shoot here, he'd run. Remember the safety gadget on the door this time. . . .

The amber changed to red before them. A convulsion of hope ran through her, she sat forward very slightly, bracing herself, as the car slowed and rolled up to the lights. And suddenly there was the stab in her side, the blunt black barrel reminding her, and the blue-ringed eyes more chilling than the gun.

"*Don't*!" he said, his right hand still gently manipulating the wheel. "You might do for me, but I should do for you first."

He had known exactly what was in her mind. Either he had foreseen it all the time, or else the slight tension of joy had communicated itself to him as clearly as if she had declared her intent aloud. And all she had out of it was one more odd fact about him: he was ambidextrous, he could shoot her as readily with the left hand as the right. Now she had the option of inviting her own death at once, or waiting for a better chance, without much conviction that there would ever be one.

What she actually did emerged not as the consequence of thought at all, but blindly, on an impulse she had no time to assess. The car was still very slowly in motion, about to brake to a halt, and Hillard was looking their way, though from across the street he had no chance of seeing and recognising her. He could, however, read off a registration number without difficulty from there, if there should be a blatant offence. . . .

She turned her head and peered back through the rear window, and in a sharp cry of vengeful delight she crowed: "There's a police car pulling up behind us! *He's getting out . . . !*"

She might have killed herself one way, but she had as nearly risked doing it in another. The driver's foot went down on the accelerator so violently that she was jerked back stunningly in her seat, wrenching her neck and setting fireworks scintillating before her eyes. Light and darkness flickered wildly past her, as the car shot across the intersection at high speed. A large Austin, crossing sedately with the lights in its favour, braked hard, a van's tyres smoked and squealed on the tarmac dry with frost. But they were through, untouched, and boring along the modestly-lit tunnel of Hawkworth Road at an illegal sixty-five. Bunty clung to the edge of the seat, gasping for the breath that had been knocked out of her, and recovered it only to break into weak, involuntary laughter, rather from relief at finding herself still alive than from any sense of achievement.

No more of that sort of thing! If she had stopped to think she would never have taken such a chance. The wonder was that the gun had not gone off in his hand when she sprang the trap; the violence of his reaction showed her how near she had come to that ending. Hair-trigger nerves might be expected in a murderer on the run. And if only he'd kept his head and looked in his mirror, instead of tramping on the accelerator the instant she had sounded the alarm, he might have got through Comerford and away without question.

"Damn you!" moaned the bitter voice beside her, shaky with fury. "*Damn you!* There wasn't any damned police car!"

"There soon will be," she said, "now."

If Hillard had missed getting their number, someone in the Austin or the van would surely have noted it. Was that anything gained? It might be, if Hillard was quick to act on it. If the fugitive was heading for the M.6 he could hardly avoid going through Hawkworth, and there would be time to alert the police there by telephone, and even to set up a road-block. There was a strong campaign on against dangerous driving, and their exit from Comerford had certainly been spectacular.

If she could work out all that, so could he. He knew the odds now, he was concentrating on getting past Hawkworth in the least possible time, but if her luck held he wouldn't be quick enough, even at this lawless speed.

At this moment she would have been certain of her own imminent death, if he had dared take a hand from the wheel or divert a thought from his driving to kill her. That was her only security, after what she had just done to him : nothing could happen to her while he was driving at this intensity. Better pray that the police would stop him at Hawkworth. If they did not, only one encouraging consideration remained, that he would surely prefer to remove her as far as possible from home before killing and disposing of her, in order to gain more time to make his own escape. Given a few hours' grace you can hide a body, even two bodies, competently enough to delay inquiries for weeks, by which time he undoubtedly meant to be far away.

Now she was nothing but a passenger, quiescent from self-interest. He still had the gun ready in his left hand, even as he held the wheel. At the next threat he could use it instantly. She sat tensed and silent, waiting for the first glimmer of the sodium lighting of Hawkworth.

They reached the well-lit approach road, and he didn't slow down. Now she could see his face by fits and starts as they passed the lamp standards, fixed like marble, in brittle, nervous lines of strain, with sweat glistening on his forehead and lip. And suddenly he was braking, but with a deliberation that promised nothing, and positioning the car well out into the centre of the road. He had seen the barrier before she had. Hillard hadn't failed her, the police had closed half the road here at the approach to the town. But only half! And he was going through, she felt it in her blood.

From behind the white trestle on the left of the road a young police constable stepped out full into their path, with his hand extended to wave them down. Bunty heard the man beside her gulp in air in a huge sob, and felt his foot go down on the accelerator.

The boy in uniform was standing confidently in the centre of the free way; his confidence in the law he represented drew a warning scream up into her throat, but she choked on it silently and could not utter a sound. She would have closed her eyes, but it was impossible, the young figure held them fixed in fascination. She saw his face leap towards her, saw it dissolve from tolerant serenity into incredulous doubt, and then into terror, as the car drove straight at him.

At the last instant the wheel swung dizzily, and was hurled impetuously back again. The constable leaped backwards, late but alive, as the car swerved round him and surged away. They missed the boy by inches, and the lamp standard on the other side by the thickness of the old car's well-maintained paint. Bunty uttered a cry, and clawed her way round to kneel on the seat and look back through the rear window; the young policeman was just getting up from the ground, and the police car that had been standing by, not expecting any trouble, was

charging off the mark after them, too late to hold them
in sight for long, unless it could better the crazy seventy-
five they were exceeding through the sleeping town.

She slid down into her seat weakly, and lay limp beside
her enemy. His eyes were dividing their attention now
about equally between the road ahead and his rear-view
mirror. He didn't ask her anything; she might not have
been there. He was nothing but a machine for driving,
and what a machine, precise, confident, dæmonic. Well,
they knew now what they had to contend with. That
attempted murder was notice enough. It was more than
a case of dangerous driving and jumping the lights now.
This pursuit would be serious. To be honest, she was
more sure that they would chase him to the ends of the
earth for trying to kill a police constable than for murder-
ing an anonymous girl.

As for her, she had lost her chance. Unless that pursuing car, just about holding its distance, managed to stop
them short of the motorway, she was as good as dead.

But between them—shouldn't he share the credit?—
they had ensured that the hunt should be up in full cry
after them.

::   ::

He shook off the police car in the country roads between
Hawkworth and the M.6. No doubt of it now, he was a
local man, or at least he'd lived here long enough to know
these roads like the palm of his hand, better than the
police driver knew them. They hit the motorway at the
quietest entrance, well away from the town, and after
that he took the fast lane and drove like an inspired devil.
Who was there to enforce the limit? It was an unreal
limit, in any case, on a clear, starlit night with visibility
equal almost to that in daylight, and little traffic on the
road. And whatever this man might or might not be, he
was a driver of exceptional gifts. They would take some
catching now.

The marvellous road unrolled, broad, generous, splen-

didly surfaced, unwinding before them in a hypnotic
rhythm. Service areas sprang up beside them in a galaxy
of lights, and passed, committing them again to the dark.
Her tired eyes began to dazzle, and then to ache inconsolably. She closed them, and instantly could see more
clearly. The ride was so calm that with closed eyes it was
possible to rest, and think, and even understand.

Almost certainly, she was going to die. It was essential
to grasp that, and to come to terms with it. She must not
expect anything better. If better was to be had, somehow she would fight her way to it; if not, she had to deal
with what was possible. Inordinately clearly she saw what
was happening to her, and it was no longer a dream, and
no longer fantastic.

After all, this sort of thing happens to other women, too,
in slightly different circumstances, but to the same ultimate
effect. Doctors tell them suddenly, after what should
have been a routine examination, that they have been
carrying malignant growths round with them unknown,
perhaps for months, perhaps for years. Symptoms come
late in the day. Or, worse, the doctors don't tell them, but
subscribe to the convention that cancer is unmentionable,
and coax them into hospital with soothing pretences that
minor treatment is necessary, and only slowly, with infinite anguish, do the victims penetrate to the knowledge
that they have been carrying the balance of life and death
within them, with all the betting on death. A mistake, to
make death the enemy. Death is the ultimate destination
of every one of us, and what's beyond remains to be seen.
But fear, doubt, delusion are the real enemies. If you
know, you have at least the chance to effect a reconcili-
ation.

She had that chance. If he had killed her at once it
might have seemed to be a mercy, but now she knew that
it would have been nothing of the kind. There was always
the last moment of realisation, the horror of knowing too
late, without time to come to terms, without one instant

to muster the last dignity. It is not death which is the violation, it is fear.

It was there within her eyelids, death, within touch of her hand, smiling at her. Already it was becoming better-known, almost familiar. It was waiting for everyone, some-where along the line, often when least expected. What's the use of claiming immunity? Of yelling at fate: Why *me*? In effect, why not me? Those who go out innocently to do their regular shopping, and inadvertently step under buses, seemed to her, strangely enough, infinitely more to be pitied.

:: ::

They were off the motorway, unchallenged, and strik-ing north still for Kendal, Penrith and Carlisle. She knew this road, she had travelled it before, and could recognise landmarks, even in the dark. There had been a long, hallucinatory interlude of half-sleep, drugged with speed and darkness and isolation. Nothing could happen to her, as long as he drove. No succour could relieve her, as long as he drove.

It was somewhere between Penrith and Carlisle that she spoke to him, softly and reasonably as to a backward and capricious child. Her own senses were dazzled with this rush through the night, she heard her voice as a stranger's, a calm, rational stranger's, arguing with un-reason.

"Murder isn't a capital crime any more, you know that? They don't hang you now."

He didn't say anything, he merely drove like a machine; she might as well not have been there.

"What you've done may not even be considered murder. If there was great provocation on her part, and loss of control on yours, they might reduce the charge. You think you're forced to kill again, now that I know, but that's an illusion. Your life isn't threatened."

He took no notice at all. Everything in him, every sense, every force, was concentrated on just one purpose, to get to wherever it was he was going, and get rid of his burden. He heard her, though, she was sure of that; he knew exactly what she was saying. He had nothing to say in reply because nothing she had said made any difference to his resolution. And she herself felt exasperatedly how futile it was to tell a young man he could keep his life and spare hers, at the cost of a mere fourteen years or so in prison! No, he wasn't interested in that prospect. He meant to get clear away, to escape undetected, and there was only one way he could hope to do that. She knew too much to be left alive. None the less, she went on trying. She had to. Acknowledging that you may have to die doesn't absolve you from putting up the devil of a fight for your life.

"And supposing they do catch up with you? They know which way you were heading, and they won't give up, you know that. There's a policeman involved now. Why make it worse for yourself if they do get you? You might get by with a plea of manslaughter for her—you won't for me!"

Her eyes had grown accustomed to the night by now, she could see clearly the outlines of the sharp profile beside her, and they remained as fixed as stone. It was like talking to a re-animated corpse that could function mechanically, but could never be reached by any human contact.

"It would be simpler to ditch me here. I don't know where you're going, I don't know who you are, I don't know anything about you. By the time I got to anyone, you could be miles away. And," she said reasonably, "you wouldn't have the delay and trouble of disposing of me. That might make all the difference between getting clean away and getting caught. Because you don't think I'm going to make it quick and easy for you, do you?"

Maybe she had been wrong in thinking he couldn't be reached, for the knuckles of the capable hands that lay so knowledgeably on the wheel had sharpened into pale points of tension, white as china, and his cheek-bone strained at the stretched silvery skin as if it would break through.

"And there's hardly room for two in the boot," she said viciously.

"Shut up!" he gasped in a muted howl of pain and despair. "Shut up, *damn you, shut up*!"

::   ::

The last thing she remembered recognising was the smithy at Gretna, journey's-end for so many runaway couples pursued north by this road. The irony roused her to a faint spurt of laughter. She was so drugged and lightheaded with exhaustion by then that nothing was quite real. Even fear could not keep her awake any longer. Uneasily, stiffly, she slept against her enemy's shoulder.

She awoke with a violent start, flung forward against the dashboard, fending herself off feverishly with her hands, still half-dazed and jangled between truth and illusion. He had braked violently, and for the moment that was the only reality she could grasp. Then it was like a curious dance, the car swinging first left and then right in a frustrated measure, like a man in a hurry trying to get past a slower walker on a narrow pavement. She heard the man beside her swearing furiously through his teeth as he wove this way and that. And then she saw the hare, bounding along in front of them in the middle of the road, as hares will, frantic with fear but still trusting in his speed to get him out of trouble. The car, driven with patience and precision, tried to edge him aside into the hedge-bank, and always he resisted the suggestion and raced straight ahead.

"Go on, curse you, get *out* of it!"

She looked at the light and the land outside the windows of her moving prison, and saw that it was almost morning, the air grey and still before dawn, and they were on an upland road between rolling wastes of heath, with the shadowy shapes of hills beyond, like gauzy folds of sky. If he slowed much more, she might almost dare to claw open the door and run. . . . He had pocketed the gun long ago, on the side away from her, and his eyes were on the stupid creature that loped ahead of him, he would be slow to react at this moment. But run where? There were no houses here, and little cover.

And it was too late now in any case. He had dropped back and ambled to give the hare a long enough start to feel safe, to forget the impulse to flight, and return to the heather. And there went the long ears and lolloping hind-quarters, off into the bracken under the low hedge, and out of sight. The car shot forward again in a smooth acceleration, and sailed past the spot where the creature had vanished. The needle of the speedometer crept back energetically to seventy. Since the moment when they had driven at the policeman on the edge of Hawkworth, only that hare had kept them for a few minutes within the legal speed limit.

She had no idea where they were, or how long they had now been on the road. In the chill of the dawn her sense of fear seemed to have reached a dead level where her predicament was at once disbelieved-in and accepted. She was finding out a great deal about the human mind under stress, the odd detachment and accuracy of observation of which it is capable even in terror, and the rapidity with which terror itself can become familiar, and cease to impress. You even reach, she thought, the point of contemplating without panic that there really may not be any way out; and you reach it unbelievably quickly.

The car swung sharply to the right, hardly slowing for the turn, and entered a narrow, winding, sunken lane. The air had a cold tang that made Bunty's nostrils quiver, and the trees along the ridge on their right all leaned towards them in a way there was no mistaking. Somewhere just out of sight before them lay the sea.

The miniature valley, trees leaning over it on either side on the sheltered slopes, opened in a few minutes into a broad circle of gravel before a small cottage, pink-washed over walls of stone below and brick above, with a low-pitched, overhanging roof. It had a bright, polished, cared-for look which meant that someone with money and leisure had taken it over. There was a brand-new garage to the left, tucked under the slope of grass and trees, there were modern windows, obviously installed since the take-over, and decorative shrubs had been deployed artfully among the grass to make the most manageable of gardens. Someone's pleasure place, there's no mistaking the signs. And this man knew his way about here; she recognised it from the manner in which he had taken the sharp bend into the lane, and she saw it again in the dexterity with which he swept the car round and stopped it right in front of the cottage, in such a way that on her side there was just room to open the door, and she would be stepping out practically into the porch.

The moment the engine stopped he had the gun in his hand again, ready, and in one swing he was out of the car.

"Get out. And don't try to run, you wouldn't get far."

As she straightened up stiffly after the long ride, the round black eye of the gun stared at her steadily across the roof of the car. She didn't try to run. Against the ten yards of pale wall on either side she would have been an easy mark. He came round to join her at his leisure, and taking her by the arm, put her before him into the porch, where his own bulk securely hemmed her in. He reached above him under the low roof, and swung aside a corner of the wooden beading. The key had its regular hiding-place, and he was in the secret.

"Go in, please."

The growing daylight showed her a tiny hall in spectral pastel colours, a staircase on one side, two white doors on the other, the minimum of holiday-cottage furniture, but of an elegant kind. The outer door closed behind them with a solid, final sound, and they were shut in together. She heard the key turned again in the lock, and watched him withdraw it and pocket it. And now at last he was no longer occupied with driving; his hands were free.

"Upstairs! You'll find the bathroom on the left. I'm sorry there'll be only cold water until I see to the main switch. Take your time."

It was fantastic. The automatic politeness of his up-bringing still clung to him, glaringly odd in this relation-ship. He might have been apologising to a guest for the lack of amenities, except that his voice was too dull and drained of feeling to match the words. She looked back from the door of the bathroom, and saw that he had seated himself on the stairs below, and had the gun ready in his hand still. No chances were going to be offered to her, no chances of any kind.

The back view of him was strangely desolate, the head drooping with its lank black hair dishevelled, the shoulders sagging. If she was sick with weariness, what must his exhaustion be? In the end there might be the chance he could not deny her; even he must succumb to sleep sooner or later.

She shot the bolt of the bathroom door after her, and groped for the cord of the light-switch, but nothing hap-pened. Of course, the main switch was off, somewhere down there in the back premises, and there'd be no lights until he turned it on. The window was small, and the light from outside seemed to have dwindled almost into night again, now that she saw it from withindoors. It was barely half past five, after all that nightmare journey.

The cold water was bracing and welcome, and simply to be alone there, with a door and a bolt dividing her from him, was in itself a new lease of life. Evidently this place was used frequently and always kept ready for occupation, for there was soap on the wash-basin, and towels in the small white cupboard. Neat, small guest tablets of soap that fitted admirably into the palm. She considered for a moment, and then rolled the one she had used in her handkerchief, and slipped it into her handbag. There was nothing else she could see that might be useful to her; she took her time, as he had suggested, about looking round for a weapon to use against him. She had hoped there might be a razor, at least of the safety variety, in the cabinet, and therefore blades; but of course, the owner used an electric, there was the socket for it beside the mirror. Nothing there for her. The bolt on the door was a fragile thing, if she refused to come out it wouldn't preserve her for long. There remained that window, discouragingly small and high though it was.

She carried the stool over to it, climbed up, snapped back the latch and hoisted the sash. Empty air surged away before her face. Craning over the sill to look down, she saw that on the rear side of the house the ground fell away sharply in a tumble of stones, almost a cliff, and instead of being one modest story from safe ground, she found herself peering down fifty feet of broken rock. No hope of climbing out from there.

So in the end she would have to open the door again, and go back to him. She did it very softly and cautiously, easing back the bolt without a sound, for she had left him sitting on the stairs a long time, and sleep might have instead of being one modest story from safe ground, she set foot on the landing he was on his feet, too, and turning to mount the remaining steps of the flight.

"Into the next room, please." He reached past her to open the middle door of the three. "Yes," he said, following the rapid glance she gave to the curving latch and the key-hole below it, "there's a lock. I can't afford any slips now, can I? You didn't leave me much choice."

Just over the threshold of the little bedroom, primrose and white, a charming place to house a guest, Bunty halted. With her back turned to him she said softly and deliberately:

"Do you know why I opened the boot?"

She didn't look round, but she felt, almost she scented, the effusion of his desolation, bewilderment and despair, and the ache of his amputation from the harmless creature he must once have been.

The dull voice behind her said, dragging with weariness:

"What difference does it make?"

"I was looking for a rug," she said, "to put over you."

There was one instant of absolute silence, then the door closed as abruptly as a cry, and she heard the key turned hastily, clumsily in the lock. For a long minute she caught the deep, harsh, strained accent of his breathing, close there against the door, so that almost she could see his damp forehead pressed against the cold white panelling, and the veined eyelids heavy as marble over the burned-out grey eyes. Only slowly and with infinite effort did he drag himself away; she heard his steps slur along the carpeted landing, and stumble down the stairs.

CHAPTER IV

THE FIRST THING she did was to cross to the window and hoist the sash, to have a second look at the lie of the land seawards. The bedroom looked out, like the bathroom, to the rear of the house, but not directly towards the water. To the left lay the outline of the coast above the cliffs, undulating between tree-lined hollows and blanched grassy brows, but beneath the walls of the cottage the land crumbled away towards the sea. By craning out to extend her view to the right she could see the cliffs broken by a small, tight inlet, where the tide came in to a tiny jetty and a boat-house. Many a small house like this must have been snapped up by boating enthusiasts as desirable week-end accommodation, all round the Scottish coast. Did it belong to this man's family? Surely to someone who knew him well, or he wouldn't have been admitted to all its secrets. There seemed to be a rocky path leading down from the house to the inlet, but only here and there could she glimpse a level, slated spot that formed a part of it.

The drop from the window she abandoned as impossible. Even if she had had sheets enough to knot into a rope, and confidence enough in the finished article to trust herself to it—after all, what had she to lose?—she didn't believe she could climb round the corner of the house to level ground. Forget that, and consider the contents of the room.

She was closing the window again when she heard the car below start up, and gently roll the few yards into the garage, and in a moment the double doors closed hollowly over it. Naturally he wouldn't risk leaving that where it could be seen, and draw attention to itself and him.

Well, if she couldn't get out of here, could she keep him from getting in? The trouble with modernised holiday cottages is that everything tends to be either light-weight or built-in. Wardrobe and dressing-table here were neatly contrived with white-wood shelving built on to the wall, there was nothing of any solidity that was movable, not even the bed. A child could have shoved that across the floor on its admirable and infuriating ball castors. There were no bolts inside the door to supplement the lock, and she couldn't barricade herself in.

There remained only the lock itself, new and presumably efficient, but surely also a light-weight, a token seal on privacy. She emptied the contents of her handbag on the bed, and fingered them over for anything that might provide a tool or a weapon. The obvious lock-picker was her nail-file, a giant from the lavish manicure case George had once given her, long and strong and with a formidable point. She had another use for that, however. It was the only thing she had that even suggested a weapon, all it lacked was a comfortable handle that would give her more control and force in using it, and she supplied that by embedding

the unpointed end firmly in the cake of soap she had stolen
from the bathroom. It wasn't much as defence against a
gun, but if she got a chance she intended to forestall that
direct confrontation. If she had had this in her hand half
an hour ago, when he had sat there in broken exhaustion
on the stairs, with his back turned to her . . .

So this, she thought, pushing back the tangled hair from
her forehead, this is how killers are made. No, I can't! Not
unless . . . not until . . . All the same, she fingered the point
of the file, and remembering that there were bricks outside the window, went and flung up the sash again, and
began carefully whetting the improvised dagger, first one
end, then the other, watching the scored surfaces grow
bright.

The light was growing brighter, too. She was facing to
the right, towards the sea, and the layer of mist that floated
above the water thinned before her face into diaphanous
wisps, and dissolved in light. She looked down towards the
inlet, her eyes drawn by a tiny point of colour and movement. Out of the boat-house a graceful blond shape slipped
demurely, all pale, smooth woodwork and gleaming brass
and bright blue paint, stealing along like a cat to rub itself
delicately against the jetty. Of course, how lucky for him
that he knew somebody with a secluded cottage on the
coast, and a boat that could make it, in the right hands,
over to the Low Countries. Somewhere at any rate, on
the way to a much more distant place where a man could
vanish.

He was there in the boat, she saw the thin dark figure step
ashore and make the boat fast. He was bringing something in his arms from the foot of the path. What it was
she could not see at first, though she saw him stoop to
hoist it, and could easily recognise that it was heavy, and
filled his arms. Only when he stowed it aft, and went to
drag up a tarpaulin cover over it, did she realise how simple
and significant a thing it was. A large, jagged stone. That
was all.

She stood at the window, the file arrested in her hand. Of course, that was one of the simpler essentials. He would need a weight.

No, she corrected herself, two weights. And here he came with the second one, placing it carefully, to avoid disturbing the trim of the boat. There would be two bodies, a double burial at sea. No use hiding the first without at the same time disposing of the second, and rendering it silent for ever.

She was looking on at the final preparations for her own death and burial.

: :   : :

She was probing desperately at the lock with a straightened hair-grip, two of her nails broken and a fingertip bleeding and raw, when she heard her enemy enter the house and begin to climb the stairs. The key turned in the lock; the door opened.

" Come down, when you're ready."

His voice was level and dull. His eyes, though they did not avoid her, hardly seemed to see her, but she had no doubt that they would give him notice sharply enough if she made a false move. Nor could she see the gun, but it must be ready in his pocket in case of need. The dimness on the landing sheltered him a little, turned him into a mere lay figure, a cardboard cut-out in shades of grey. She picked up her handbag from the bed, walked steadily past him to the bathroom, and bolted the door; and after a moment she heard him go slowly down the stairs, step by heavy step like a lame man.

All the time that she was in there, making up her face with almost superstitious care to get everything right, and with a flat, dream-like sense of saying good-bye, she could feel his eyes down below, never swerving from the staircase, penning her in. When she had done her extended best for her appearance she would have to go down and face him. You can't just crouch in a corner and close your eyes, and wait for a miracle. She made sure that her makeshift dagger was disposed at the right angle at the top of the jumbled possessions in her bag, with a fold of her handkerchief covering it. If you have to go down, you go down fighting.

Sunday morning breakfast she thought numbly, on a brief week-end jaunt before the winter sets in! Where was I yesterday? Safe at home in all that autumnal oppression, with nothing to do but wait for everything to be all right again. If it had been a clear, sunny morning like this, nothing need ever have happened, all those cobwebs would have melted from me like mist. She counted the years now, and they were nothing, a triviality, dropped petals, with illimitable wealth still to fall. She took her sights from the past resolutely, and set them on the shrunken future.

With a step as slow and drugged as his, she went down the stairs; and he was there, as she had known he would be, waiting for her. He held open the second white door in the hall. The living-room of this spectacular little house would obviously be designed to overlook the sea. A remnant of curiosity remained to her. She looked round the room with remote, unreal interest. There was a picture window, with the dawn sun framed in it in impossible beauty, for they were looking almost due east. There was a narrow white door beside it, no doubt leading into a tiny, built-in kitchenette. Everything was white wicker and orange corded silk, bright, inexpensive and gay, cushioned chairs, a light settee, a small dining-table with an orange-coloured cloth.

Her sense of unreality grew extreme. There must be a store of non-perishable and tinned foods left in the cottage. He had made tea, and produced tinned ham, cheese and crispbread. For himself, no doubt, and he must have needed it, but he had laid two places. Either he was gone beyond the boundary of reason, or the cottage exerted on him the compulsions to which he was accustomed within its walls, and the first of them was hospitality, even to his victim.

She lost touch with her own destiny then, the unreality of that room was too much for her. She knew the facts, she knew what they predicted, but she could no longer behave in accordance with what she knew. Beyond a certain point you abandon carefulness, because it is so patently of no more use, and silence, because it makes no difference any more, and because caprice may by some freakish chance hit the jackpot you'll never get by taking aim. She began to range the room, paying no attention to him, examining everything that bore witness to the absent owners. And there on the small white bookcase, stocked with Penguins and other paperbacks for their guests, was their double photograph, a studio portrait of man and wife in their comfortable fifties, he in white open-necked shirt and silk scarf, with a round, amiable face and receding hair, she in the ageless Paisley silk shift, with a modish new shingle and a good-humoured middle-aged smile.

"Your parents?" she asked with deliberate malice; for she was quite sure that they were not his parents.

"Friends," said the heavy voice behind her. "Louise is my godmother," he added, with shattering calm.

"Ah, so that's why you're so at home here," she said. "What's their name?"

"Alport. Reggie and Louise Alport." Why care enough now to make secrets of these details? He answered her because it would have taken more energy and effort to keep silence than to speak. "If you want some tea," he said remotely, "help yourself."

She turned to look at him then, and even came to the table and sat down, suddenly aware how desperately she wanted some tea. The suggestion of the laid table was too strong to be resisted, even though all this was a pointless interlude on the way to something else, something final.

"Do they live in Comerbourne, too?"

"No, in Hereford." A dreary and desperate wonder sat upon him; and now that she saw him in the full light from the eastern window he was pale and insubstantial as paper, perished paper, so brittle that it might crumble to dust at any moment. "That's where my family come from."

"Then you work in Comerbourne." She could not have explained why it was so important to keep talking, to keep drinking tea, and swallowing mouthfuls of sawdust food that stuck in her throat; to maintain, not a pretence, but a hypnotic suggestion, that everything here was normal, and had to be preserved, so that scoring through its normality with an act of violence should be increasingly difficult. Nor could she have said why a grain of information added to her knowledge of him should seem to add to her meagre resources. The nail-file was surely a better bet. Yet she persisted. Of course, who else enjoys even one October week-end lasting until Wednesday morning? It was the half-term break; she ought to have known. "You teach," she said, feeling her way, "at one of the schools in Comerbourne."

"I did," he said distantly.

"What did you teach?"

"Art . . . if it matters now."

I wonder, she thought, feeling the shuddering undertones beneath these exchanges, whether he knows what I'm thinking as clearly as I know what's going on inside him? Kill me here and now, and he'll have the trouble of carrying or dragging me down to the boat, and the risk of being seen at it. Make me walk there to be killed on board, and he takes the chance that I may try breaking away, even at the last moment. Why not, with nothing to lose? The whole thing *could* go wrong then, even if it's an outside chance. I *might* survive to talk. No, he'll want to make sure. It will be here!

He's just made up his mind!

"How odd," she said, her eyes holding his across the table, her right hand in the open handbag on her lap, "to think that I don't even know your name."

"Why should you?" he said. And suddenly he set both

hands against the edge of the table, and pushed back his chair. His face was more dead than alive, blue-stained at lips and eyes, cemetery clay, but he moved with method and certainty, like a machine.

" Yes, what are you waiting for?" she blazed abruptly, on her feet with the nail-file in her hand. Her handbag went one way, her handkerchief another. " Do you think I don't know you've got everything ready? Even the stone for my feet?"

He got up slowly and started round the corner of the table after her, hooking a hand under the edge to hoist it aside from between them. She caught the brief reflection of light from eyes opaque and dead as grey glass.

" I'm sorry!" said the distant voice, from somewhere far beyond sorrow. " What can I do? You shouldn't have looked in there. What choice have you left me? I *liked* you," he said, wrenching at his own unavailing pain, " you were *kind* to me! But what can I do about it now?"

" You could let me walk to my grave," she said, backing from him inch by inch, " and save yourself trouble." Anything to spin out five more minutes, three, even one, to give time one more chance. And still, at this extremity, she had a corner of her mind free to wonder where the gun was, why it wasn't in his hand. He couldn't be afraid of the shot being heard, not here, there was no other dwelling in sight. If he'd had the sense to use the gun he needn't even have come within her reach, she would have had no chance at all.

His hand swung the table round, shedding the tea-pot from its tilted edge, and drove it hard against the wicker arm-chair beside the wall. She dared not turn her head to look, but her hip rammed hard into the arm of the chair, and she could retreat no farther.

" Not you," she heard his voice saying hopelessly, " you'd run, you'd swim for it, *I know you.* Why did it have to be *you*?"

Bracing her fingers round the hilt of her dagger, she had

just time to feel one angry stab of amusement, involuntary
and painful, at his appropriation of what should surely
have been her question. And then the moment and he were
on her together.

He took the last yard in one fast, light step, and reached
for her with long hands crooked; and she stooped under his
grasp instead of leaning back from him, and slashed upwards at his throat with all her weight, uncoiling towards
him like a spring. She felt the impact, and sudden heat
licked her fingers, but in the same instant he had her by
the wrist, and had wrenched hand and weapon away from
his grazed neck, forcing her arm back until her grip relaxed. Distantly, through the roaring in her ears, she heard
the nail-file tinkle on the wood blocks of the floor, a light,
derisory sound. Then his groping hands found their hold
on her throat, and chaotic eruption of light and darkness
blinded her eyes.

She put up her hands and clawed at her murderer's face,
until the pressure on her throat grew to an irresistible terror,
and then an agony, and she could only fight feebly to drag
his hands away. Her eyes burned, quite darkened now,
there was nothing left in existence but a panic struggle for
breath. A sound like sobbing thudded in her ears, the great
breaths she could no longer drag into her lungs seemed to
pulse through her failing flesh from some other source.
Someone else was dying with her, she heard him in extremity, moaning and whining with pain, and long after
she had no voice left to complain with, that lamentable
sound followed her down into darkness and silence.

: :   : :

Consciousness began again in an explosion of fiery pain;
the red-hot band of steel round her neck expanded, burst,
disintegrated. She was dead, she must be dead. Or why the
delirious cool rush of air into her body again at will, the
abrupt withdrawal of pressure and fear, the sudden wild
awareness of relief and ease? Nothing was holding her any
more, nothing confined her, her own limp hands wandered

freely to touch her bruised throat. Her knees gave way under her slowly, she slid down against the arm of the wicker chair, and collapsed into the cushions like a disjointed doll, and lay gulping in air greedily, tasting it as never before, experiencing it as a sensuous delight. The darkness lifted slowly. She opened her eyes, and colours and shapes danced dazzlingly before them. She saw sunlight reflected on the ceiling, and a shimmer that was the refractions of broken light from the motion of the sea.

Her eyes and her mind cleared together, into an unbelievable, unprecedented clarity. She lay still for a long moment, seeing the outlines of things round her with a brilliant intensity that was painful to her eyes after the darkness. The same room, the same signs of struggle, the fallen handbag on the floor, the broken tea-pot, the tablecloth dragged into disorderly folds. She was alive, she was intact. Not because of any miraculous intervention, but for solid reasons, in pursuit of which her mind stalked in silence within her recovering body. The clarity within there was as blinding and sharp as the clarity without.

She sat up slowly, clinging to the edge of the table, and looked round for her murderer.

Head-down in a dark huddle on the wicker settee, he lay clutching the orange-coloured cushions to his face with frantic energy, fingers, wrists, forearms corded with strain, as if he willed never to show himself to the light again. He had withdrawn from her the full width of the room when he snatched his hands away. Shuddering convulsions shook through him from head to foot; a touch, and he would fly apart and bleed to death. He was bleeding now, she saw the oblique graze on his neck oozing crimson, and staining the orange silk. Who had come nearer to killing?

It was at that moment that the black dolphin knocker on the front door banged peremptorily three times on its curling cast-iron wave.

CHAPTER V

THE MAN HUDDLED on the settee lay utterly still, the tremors suppressed by force, his breath held. He did not raise his head; he wanted never to raise it again. It was Bunty who dragged herself up out of her chair and went into action. She could move, she was in command of herself. And she knew what she was doing, now. Hurriedly she stooped for her handbag, and ran a comb through her hair. Would there be marks on her throat? Not yet, probably, but she shook out her chiffon scarf and tucked it in around her neck to make certain of being unremarkable. There was blood on her fingers; she dipped her handkerchief into the nearest liquid, which was the spilled tea on the table, and wiped the stains away.

" Give me the key!"

Speech hardly hurt at all. She had time to realise, even in that moment, how little she was damaged. He must have snatched his hands away from her as soon as he felt her pain.

He lifted his head at the sharp sound of her voice, and turned upon her a blind, mute face.

" The key, quickly! Give it to me!"

He sat up and felt through his pockets for it numbly, and held it out to her without a word. From his last safe place at the end of despair, where there is nothing left to lose or gain, he watched her walk out of the room, leaving the door open behind her. He heard the bolts of the front door drawn back, heard the key turned in the lock.

In those few yards Bunty lived through a total reassessment of everything that had happened to her. Her senses were abnormally acute, her mind moved with rapidity and certainty. She remembered things observed at the time without comprehension, and made sense of them. Her

62

legs might be shaky under her, but mentally she was on her feet again.

She opened the door of the cottage with the accurately measured reserve of a woman alone, knocked up at an unusually early hour on a Sunday morning. Not too wide at first, ready to close it and slip the bolt again quickly if she didn't like the look of her visitor; then surprised and relieved, setting it wide and coming confidently into the doorway.

The two uniformed policemen on the step of the porch gazed back at her in silence for a moment, more surprised to see her than she was to see them.

"Good morning!" said Bunty, and waited with the polite, questioning curiosity of the innocent to hear what they wanted of her.

"Good morning, ma'am!" The elder of the two shoved up his flat cap civilly on the furze-bush of his pepper-and-salt hair, and eyed her with circumspection, plainly finding her of a reassuring respectability. "Sorry if we startled you, but we saw a light in one of the windows here a while since, from up the coast road a piece, and knowing that the lady and gentleman who summer here have left, we wondered . . . You never know, just as well to check up, when a house is empty."

"Oh, I *see*! Yes, of course, and how very good of you! Reggie and Louise will be so grateful," said Bunty warmly, "to know that you keep such a good watch on their place. I'm a friend of the Alports, they've lent me their cottage for a long week-end. I drove up last night."

"Ah, that accounts for the light, then." He seemed to be perfectly satisfied, and why shouldn't he, when she produced the owners' names so readily? An Englishwoman of forty, dressed in a smart and rather expensive grey jersey suit, must seem probable enough as an acquaintance of the Alports; indeed, it was unlikely that such a person would ever find her way to this spot unless directed by the owners. "And you found everything in order here, ma'am? No signs of anyone prowling around in the night? No trouble at all?"

The younger policeman, tall and raw-boned, and surely a local boy, had drawn back out of the porch, and was using his eyes to good purpose without seeming to probe. The front window, through which he had already taken a sharp look, would show him only a room where everything must be as the Alports had left it. He was eyeing the hard gravel, too, but all it would tell him was that a car had arrived here, stood a little while before the door, and then been put sensibly away in the garage, which is exactly what one would expect the English lady to do with her car on arrival. Now he was turning his blue and innocent regard upon Bunty, and taking her in from head to foot, without apparent question of her genuineness, rather with a degree of critical pleasure on his own account.

"Trouble?" said Bunty, wide-eyed. Her smile faded into faint anxiety, nicely tempered with curiosity. "No, nobody's been here. Everything was all right when I arrived. Why, is something wrong?"

"Och, nothing for you to worry about, ma'am," said the sergeant comfortably. "You're no' likely to be troubled here. Most like he's gone on northwards."

"He?" she echoed. "You mean there's somebody you're looking for? A criminal?"

"We've had warning to look out for a car, ma'am, a large old car, black, thought to be a Rover, registration NAQ 788. It's known to have driven north out of England during the night. Constable at Muirdrum believes he saw the same car go past about three hours ago, heading for Arbroath, but he's no' sure of the number. We're checking up and down all these roads, just in case. But there's no call for you to worry, ma'am, you'll be fine here."

So no one, it seemed, was looking for her just yet. No one had mentioned that there'd been a woman aboard, most likely no one knew. Obviously they knew it hadn't been a woman driving.

"NAQ 788," she repeated thoughtfully. "A black Rover. I could get in touch with you if I do see anything of it, of course."

"Ay, you could do that, ma'am. But I don't think you're likely to catch sight of him, I doubt he's as far north as he can get by now."

"What do you want him for?" Bunty asked inquisitively. A woman without curiosity would be suspect anywhere. "Has he run somebody down, or something?"

"Well, no' just that!" She hadn't expected a direct answer, and clearly she wasn't going to get one, but his business-like, unalarmed attitude told her most of what she needed to know. "Constable somewhere down south had a narrow squeak, though," he vouchsafed, after due consideration. And that was all she was going to get out of him; but it seemed that he had given a second thought to getting something out of her in exchange.

"We'll be on our way then. Sorry if we disturbed you. And by the way, maybe I should have your name and home address, ma'am, just for information."

She hadn't been expecting that, but she was equal to it. Startled by her own readiness, she responded without hesitation : "I'm Rosamund Chartley—that's *Mrs.* Chartley, of course . . ." The young one, if not the other, had long since assimilated the significance of her ring. "And I live at 17 Hampton Close, Hereford." She couldn't be sure how much he would know in advance about the Alports, but her use of their name had registered immediately, she might as well play for safety and assume that he knew their home town, too. She watched him write down her instant fiction, and smiled at him as he put his note-book away; not too encouragingly, on the contrary, with a slight intimation that if that was all she could do for him she would like to go back to her interrupted breakfast.

"Thank you, ma'am, we won't keep you any longer now. And I'm sure ye needna be at all uneasy. Good morning, Mrs. Chartley!"

He re-adjusted his cap on the grizzled heather he wore
for hair, summoned his subordinate with a flick of a finger,
and they departed. She closed the door, and leaned back
against it for a moment, listening. They had a car, they
must have turned it on the gravel and withdrawn it into
the shelter of the trees before knocking at the door. She
heard it start up and wind away into the convolutions of
the lane. Only then did she re-bolt and lock the door, and
go back into the living-room.

The young man was sitting bolt upright on the settee,
dark against the brilliance and shimmer of the sea, every
nerve at stretch, his eyes fixed wildly on the empty doorway, waiting for her to reappear there. The gun was in
the clenched right hand that lay on his knee, and his
finger was crooked on the trigger.

She saw it instantly, and instantly understood. He must
have lowered his hand in sheer stupefaction when the
meaning of that astonishing performance of hers penet-
rated his mind, with his death only the tightening of a
nerve away.

Oh, God, she thought, suppose he hadn't waited to hear?
Why didn't I take it from him before I went to the door?
But there'd been no time to consider everything. And
thank God, he *had* waited, and confusion and bewilderment
had kept him from dying. Or curiosity, perhaps, curiosity
can be a valid reason for going on living, when no other
is left.

So the first thing she had to do, without delay but without any hasty gesture that could startle him back into despair, was to cross the room to him, and gently take the
thing out of his hand. He didn't resist; his cramped
fingers opened at her touch, and gave it up without protest. Enormous eyes, cloudy with wonder, devoured her
face and had no attention for anything else.

"*Why?*" he asked, in a rustling whisper.

"You won't need it now," she said. But she knew that
was not what he meant.

"Why didn't you bring them in and give me up? *Why didn't you tell them I tried to kill you?*"

: :   : :

Without a word in answer, she opened a drawer of the little writing-desk on the other side of the room, and thrust the gun far back out of sight. Then she came back to the settee and sat down beside him.

"Look," she said urgently, "you and I have got to talk. We've got a little time now, and the car's safest where it is. They won't come looking for it here now—not yet!"

"But *why did you send them away?*"

"Never mind that. There are things I've got to know, and we may not have all that long. That girl in the car— *who is she?*"

"Her name's Pippa Gallier," he said, with the docility of despair, shock and hopeless bewilderment, but with some positive motion of faith, too, as though she had surprised him into drawing back the first of the bolts that sealed his terrible solitude from the world. "We were going to be married. I *thought* we were . . ."

"She's a Comerbourne girl? That *is* where you teach, isn't it? What was she? What did she do?"

"She worked at the big fashion shop, Pope Halsey's, and did a bit of modelling for them when they had dress shows. She was an assistant buyer. She wasn't a Comerbourne girl, though, her family belong to Birmingham. She had a little flat over one of the shops in Queen Street. Why?" he asked dully, but at least there was a grain of life in his voice now, and in his eyes, that never wavered from searching her face. He had some kind of stunned trust in her now that told him she must have a reason for probing these irremediable things. Nothing she did was wanton; it didn't follow that she could change anything.

"And how did she come to die?"

"I shot her," he said, staring through her and seeing the girl's dead face.

"All right, you shot her! But that's not what I want.

I want to know how it happened, every detail, everything you remember. Tell me about it."

He drew breath as if the effort cost him infinite labour, and told her, fumbling out the sequence of events with many pauses. He was terribly tired, and completely lost, but he was still coherent.

" I wanted to marry her. We were running about to-gether steadily, until about a couple of months ago, and we were as good as engaged. And then she got very off-hand with me, for some reason, and started pulling away. She turned down dates, or she rang up to make excuses, and if I objected she flared up and walked out. They'd always tried to tell me she had other men on a string, too. . . . I never believed it. I was daft about her. . . ."

" They?" said Bunty, pouncing on this lack of definition. " Who were *they*?"

" The chap who shares—shared—my cottage, Bill Reynolds, he teaches at the same school. Other friends of ours, too."

" And some of them knew her well? Could they have been on her string themselves?"

" I don't know. I don't think so. They knew her, but not that well. I never believed it. And then just over a week ago it seemed as if we'd got past the bad patch. You know how it can be, everything straightens out and starts running on wheels. She was the sweetest I've ever known her, and things were back as they used to be. I bought her a ring. She'd never let me get that far before. I was *happy*! You know what I mean? I'd never believed there was anything wrong about her, but I'd never felt sure of her before, and now I did, she'd promised, and we were engaged. And then she suggested that we should go to London together this half-term. . . ."

" To London?" said Bunty sharply. " *Not* up here, then?"

" No, to London. She had a few days of her holiday left to use, she suggested we should drive down on Friday evening. So when it came to Friday evening I was ready well ahead of the time we'd fixed, and I ran the car round into town, to her flat, to pick her up. It was a good half-hour earlier than she'd be expecting me. And I was just parking the car, a bit away from the house—you know what it's like trying to find anywhere to park in Comerbourne—when I saw her come out of the private door of her flat. Not alone, with a fellow I'd never seen before. And she was hanging on his arm and chattering away to him and looking up into his face, like . . . like a cut-price call-girl! You can't mistake it when you do see it."

" Did they see you?" asked Bunty intently.

"No, I told you, I could only find a place farther along the street. No, they didn't see me. . . ."

"And you didn't go after them? You didn't challenge them?"

" I never had time. I'd just got out of the car when they came out, and they turned the other way. He had a car parked there just in front of the shop, and they got into it and drove off in the other direction. By the time I was across the road they were turning the corner out of Queen Street."

" What sort of car was it? Would you know it again?"

" I didn't get the number, I never thought of it, but it was a light-grey Jag. Does it matter?"

" It matters," she said sharply. " Every detail matters. What about the man?"

" I'd know him again," he said bitterly. " A big chap, well-dressed, over-dressed for Comerbourne, you don't see many dinner jackets around in Queen Street. But he made everything he had on look like slightly sporty wear, this type. You could imagine him rally-driving in a special one-off, instead of rolling round in a Jag. He had this he-man touch, and yet everything about him was smooth, his clothes, his movements . . . everything except his face. That had some pretty crude, craggy lines, a knubby forehead, auburn hair growing low, cleft chin, eyes buried in a lot of bone. Yes, I'd know *him* again!"

"And she went with him willingly? You're sure?"

"Willingly? Gladly! You should have seen her!"

"And what did you do?"

"What could I do? They were gone, and I didn't know where. But it was pretty safe betting she wasn't going to be hurrying back within the next half-hour to meet me. I went back home, trying to kid myself there must be another answer, persuading myself there'd be a message for me. And there was! Bill was just rushing off for his own half-term, to his parents' place in Essex, when I got back. He told me there'd been a phone call for me from Pippa, he'd left me a note. She was terribly sorry, but she'd have to put off leaving for our jaunt until to-morrow evening. Her mother'd turned up unexpectedly, meaning to stay overnight, and she hadn't the heart to run out on her, and couldn't even tell her she'd had a trip planned, because Mother would be so upset at having spoiled it for her! So would I mind keeping away until to-morrow evening, and she'd come along and join me as soon as she'd seen her visitor off home! And it could all have been true," he said bleakly, staring into the past with the sick fascination of one contemplating disasters about which nothing can now be done, "if I hadn't known beforehand that her visitor wore a dinner jacket and stood about six feet three in his shoes. Because we'd only just got engaged, and her mother knew nothing about me yet, and we wouldn't have wanted to spring it on her in circumstances like that, without any preparation. It could all have been true, only I knew now that there wasn't a word of truth in it.

"So I went out and got horribly drunk. Black, vicious, murderous drunk. I don't usually drink much, but I seem to have an abnormally high tolerance, it takes a lot to fill me up. But I wasn't too tight to walk round by her flat after the pubs closed, and I wasn't too far gone to know what I was seeing, either. The grey Jaguar was parked discreetly round the corner in the mews. Mother stayed the night, all right!"

"And this was Friday? But if she'd ditched you, and if you'd written her off as a dead loss, how did you come to tangle with her again on Saturday?" demanded Bunty.

"You forget, *she* didn't know I'd written her off. She thought she only had to drop me a message, and I'd swallow it whole and sit back until she wanted me again."

"Of course," she said, enlightened, "she turned up on Saturday evening according to programme!"

"According to *her* programme. And if you'll believe me, that possibility had simply never occurred to me. I was so full up with what had happened, the thing was so completely finished for me, that I'd clean forgotten she didn't know I knew! She thought everything was serene, and she only had to stroll in at my place and say: Darling, here I am, all ready! and I'd run to fetch the car, and we could start. So that's what she did, around seven o'clock on Saturday evening, came rolling up in a taxi with her biggest suitcase, and started on another apology for Friday's hold-up as soon as she came in at the door. And I'd been howling like a dog all morning with the hangover of a lifetime, and topping it up again in self-defence most of the afternoon, and I was fit for murder."

"You do realise," said Bunty, frowning with concentration, "that so far you haven't so much as mentioned that you owned a gun? Legally or illegally!"

"I didn't own a gun. Legally or illegally. I'd never had one in my hands, as far as I can remember. I know damn-all about the things. When I do mention it you're not going to believe me. I wouldn't believe myself."

"I might, though," said Bunty. "All right, get to it your own way. She came breezing in, expecting to be taken to London. And you told her that she'd had it, that it was over, and she might as well go home."

"What I told her was meaner than that, but let it go, it added up to much the same. I asked if her mother had slept well, and whether I could have the name of her tailor. She was always quick on the uptake, Pippa, not as clever as she thought she was, perhaps, but pretty sharp, all the same. She got it in a moment that I'd seen them, and she came up with a good story faster than you'd ever credit. That was her mother's cousin, that man with the Jaguar, it was because he'd turned up for a visit that her mother'd been able to make the trip, and that's why she had no warning. And she was all set to put me in the wrong and herself in the right, as usual, and *I* was the one who was supposed to apologise. Only this time it didn't 'work. Damn it, I'd *seen* them! I asked her whether they'd locked Mother in the flat while they went out to dinner, because I'd seen her just slipping her keys in her bag. You're a liar, I told her, and a cheat, and what else you are you know best, but as far as I'm concerned, I've done with you, you can go to London, or the devil, or wherever you please, *but not with me*. She couldn't believe it. I'd been so easy up to then, it took a little while to sink in. But as soon as she did manage to get it into her head that I meant it, things got even crazier than they already were. She started persuading, threatening, even fawning . . . you've no idea how fantastic a performance that was, from Pippa. You'd have thought getting to London that night was a matter of life and death to her. She'd expected the car to be waiting in the road for her, and instead, it was locked in the garage Bill and I rent —rented—down at Floods', at the end of the street. When she realised nothing was going to get her her own way any more, she suddenly dived her hand into her bag and pulled out a gun. *That* gun." He glanced across at the drawer where Bunty had hidden it, and then at her attentive face, and said wryly : " I told you you wouldn't believe me."

She gave him no reassurances, and made him no promises. Not yet. " Go on," she said.

" Well, I still can't believe in it myself. These things don't happen, not in connection with people like Pippa. Where would she get a gun? Why should she want one?

And why, for God's sake, should she care enough about going to London with me to grab it out of her bag and point it at me, and tell me I'd better keep my promise to drive her down, or else! Why? It mattered to her just getting her own way, I know, but surely not *that* much? And she meant it, I know she did, now. But then . . ."

"Then," said Bunty, "you were too furious to be cautious."

"Too drunk," he said hardly. "She waved this thing at me, and threatened, and as far as I was concerned that was the last straw. I *wanted* to kill her . . . or, at least, I was ready to. Oh, I know that, all right! When it happens to you, you know it. I just went for her. No holds barred. I got her by the wrist and we had a wild, untidy sort of struggle for the gun. About the rest I'm not sure. But I *know* I ripped it out of her hand. I *know* that. I know *I* was holding it when we both fell over together, and went down with a crash. I'm not sure what I hit. The edge of the table, I think. I hit something, all right, I've still got the hell of a headache and a bump like a hen's egg to prove it. All I know for certain is that I went out cold for a time. I don't know how long, exactly, but not long, not more than twenty or twenty-five minutes, I'd say. When I came round, I was lying over Pippa on the floor. And I still had the gun in my hand. And Pippa . . . she was dead. It took me a few minutes to understand that. I was shaking her, talking to her, telling her playing the fool wouldn't get her anything. . . . Oh, my God! You wouldn't believe how little different she looked . . . not different at all. There was no blood, nothing to show for it, only that small hole in her sweater. She looked just as if she was pretending, to frighten me. And that would have been like her, too. But she didn't move, and she didn't breathe . . . and there was that hole, and just the ooze of blood round it, that her sweater absorbed. And in the end I knew she was dead, really dead, and I'd killed her. You," he said abruptly, turning the full devastating stare of his haggard eyes on Bunty, "you change things. But not even you can change that."

She leaned forward and laid her hand possessively on his arm, holding him eye to eye with her. "The shot. . . . There's just one bullet-hole. Did you hear the shot?"

He thought that over with agonised care. "Not that I can remember. I'd expect the moment when we fell to be the moment when the gun went off. When I fired it," he corrected himself grimly. "I told you, I meant murder. But I don't actually remember hearing the shot. All I know beyond doubt is that I came round, and she was dead.

"And I panicked. I can't blame the drink for that. I wasn't in very good shape when I came round, but I tell you, I was stone cold sober. I tidied up the room, and locked the house, and ran for the car. You can get it round to the back gate, and it's quite private there. I packed up girl and luggage and all in the boot, and picked up the spent cartridge case—it was there on the floor right beside her—and locked the place up again, as if we'd set off according to plan, and got out of there. It didn't take long, there was no mess, no blood . . . She was lying on her back, you see, and I reckon the bullet must be still in her, I couldn't find any exit wound. I threw the spent case in a field as soon as I was out of town. All I thought of was getting away. At first I didn't know where, I was driving round and round on the country roads in a state of shock, trying to think, and I had to have a drink to help me. I *had* to. And that was when I met you."

He looked up, and for a moment studied her with wonder and care, forgetting himself. "It's funny, how you've changed. You had the black dog on you then, too. It was because you were sad that I wanted to talk to you. I wish I'd left you alone. I'm sorry!"

"What were you going to do?" asked Bunty.

"I thought of this place. I've been here several times with Reggie and Louise, and they gave me an open invitation to use it even after they'd packed it in for the year and gone home. They're like that, they probably invited other people, too. That's why they leave a key. And I thought of Reggie's boat."

"You were going to drop her overboard," said Bunty, " and head for Denmark, or somewhere. . . ."

"Norway, actually. It must be possible to land un-observed somewhere on all that tremendous coastline, and I know my way around there a little. I've even got friends there . . . though I don't suppose," he owned drearily, " that I could have dragged them into this mess."

"And I," she said practically, almost cheerfully, " was to go overboard, too, in mid-passage."

He stared back at her mutely, out of the extremes of exhaustion, unable any longer to be ashamed or afraid. Even the tension which had held him upright was broken now, after the slow blood-letting of this confession. He was close to total collapse.

"Why didn't you take your chance when it came?" he asked in a thread of a voice. " Why did you send the police away?"

She got up slowly, and moved away from him to pick up the shards of the tea-pot. " I'd better get this mess cleaned up," she said, momentarily side-tracked, and lost that thread again on the instant. The housewife was there, somewhere inside, but fighting against the odds. She straightened up with the fragments in her hands, and stood frowning down at them thoughtfully.

"I didn't need them," she said, and turned to face the boy on the settee, whose eyes had never ceased their faith-ful study of her through the cloud of their guilt and sorrow and resignation.

"I'd only just realised it," she said deliberately, " but I knew I didn't need them. In the night I wasn't thinking or noticing very clearly, or I might have known before. Things are distorted as soon as you're afraid. Maybe I did know, subconsciously. I think I may have done. I had all the evidence, if I'd been able to recognise it. When you

drove at that constable in Hawkworth . . . did he jump
back first, or did you swerve first? I didn't work it out
then, I know now. And what a lot of trouble you went to,
to avoid running down a hare, even when *you* were on the
run. No wonder you couldn't go through with it when it
came to my turn."

Half of that, she realised, was lost upon him. He was in
no condition to follow her through such a maze; but he
clung to his own question, and it bore a slightly different
inflection now, tinted with the living wonder of genuine
curiosity, and—was it possible?—hope!

"Why did you send them away? Why didn't you hand
me over to them, and be safe?"

"Because," said Bunty, now with something very like
certainty, "I *was* safe. Because I don't believe you are a
murderer. I don't believe you ever killed anyone, *not even
Pippa*!"

CHAPTER VI

FOR A LONG MOMENT he stared up at her in absolute
stupefaction, hardly able to grasp what she had said, and
even when his battered mind had got hold of the words, the
sense was too slippery and elusive to be mastered without
a struggle. She saw his lips moving automatically over the
incredible syllables, and understanding came in a late, dis-
ruptive agony, and set him shaking again.

"My God, I wish that was even possible," he said, panting, "but it's crazy. Look, there were only two characters
in all this lousy scene, Pippa and me. Nobody else! Don't
you start kidding me along at this stage. It's nice of you
even to pretend to believe I might be human, after all I've
done to you, but . . ."

"I'm not pretending," she said strongly. "That's what I
do believe. Time's short, I can't spare any for kidding you

along, and you can't spare any for having doubts about me, if we're going to make anything of this mess."

"*Make* anything of it?" he echoed incredulously. "For God's sake, what is there left to make, except restitution?"

"We could begin by making sense of what we know. *Know,* not assume."

He clutched helplessly at his head, squeezed his thin grey cheeks hard between his hands, and shook himself till the lank dark hair flopped on his forehead; but when he opened his eyes again and stared up at her dizzily until her image cleared, she was still confronting him with the same fixed and resolute face.

"Don't!" he said piteously. "Not unless you mean it! I was just coming to terms with what I am. If you start me hoping now it only means I've got to go through this hell twice over. I couldn't stand it! *What we know!* I know I was lying on top of her, and she was dead with a bullet in her, and I was clutching the gun. I know I got it out of her hand, I know I was holding it when we fell. I know I wanted to kill her. . . ."

"You wanted to kill me," said Bunty bluntly. "What does that prove?"

"No," he said passionately, "I never *wanted* to kill *you.* I *meant* to. . . ."

"Meant to or wanted to, I'm still here."

"But there was no one else there, only the two of us. . . ."

"*How do you know that? You were out for twenty minutes.*"

"You *do* mean it," he said, staring, and quaked with his sudden devouring hope and fear. He dared not believe that there was anything in this intuition of hers, but it was an impossibility to doubt the genuineness of her conviction. He began to want his innocence with an agonising intensity.

"But if I didn't kill her, who did? Who else had my motive? Who else had a motive at all?"

"How can we know that, when we know next to nothing about her? If she was betraying you she could have been betraying others as well. And if it was a sound motive for you, so it was for them."

"But how could any of them even know where she was? She came in a taxi. *I* was *there*, motive and all. The most I could squeeze out of it," he said wretchedly, "was that it might have been almost an accident, when it came to the point . . . that the gun might have gone off when we fell. Even that I couldn't make myself believe. So if that's what you're trying to prove. . . ."

"No," she said at once, "not that. Because I think murder *was* done that evening. *But not by you*."

"I wish to God," he said, trembling, "you could convince me."

"Give me a chance to try. Let me look at that bump of yours, where you hit the table—if you did hit the table."

He sat charmed into obedient stillness as she took his head in her hands and turned him a little to get the full light from the window on the place. She felt his lean cheeks, cold with his long weariness, flush into warmth and grow taut with awareness of her touch. His eyes, which he had closed at her approach, as a measure of his devoted docility, opened suddenly and looked up at her, moved and dazzled. For the first time she realised how young he was, surely three or four years short of thirty. She was looking at an over-wrought boy, who had delivered himself into her hands, now absolutely defenceless. And she had promised him a miracle! Miracles are not easy to deliver; she trembled with him as she thought of her responsibility.

"It's crazy," he said, shivering. "After all this, I don't even know what to call you."

"Most people call me Bunty. Bend your head forward . . . that's it."

The mark of the blow he had taken was there to be found without difficulty, a swollen, tender pear-shape, above and if anything slightly behind his right ear. The forward end of it was higher, and only there was the skin slightly broken in one spot. She parted the thick dark hair to examine the mark carefully.

"I'm not a doctor, or even a nurse. But unless you've got a table with padded edges, it certainly wasn't the table that did this. If you'd hit any sharp edge you'd have had a considerable cut."

"There's an old wooden-framed chair with leather upholstery," he said indistinctly from under the fall of tangled hair. "It was close by the table, on my right. Not the overstuffed kind, you'd feel the wood underneath, all right, if you fell on it. It could have been the back of that."

"It could . . . but you'd have had to fall sideways . . . or else to turn your head sharply as you fell. You've got a diagonal welt, like this. . . ." She drew her fingers along it, and their course ended decidedly behind his ear. "It looks to me much more the kind of mark you'd have if someone had come up behind you and hit you one nice, scientific tap to put you out for the count. And somebody who knew how to go about it, and had the right sort of tool for the job." She smoothed back his hair over the tender place, and came round the arm of the couch to face him. "Maybe a piece of lead piping inside a sock," she said. She was smiling, faintly but positively. "Or more likely the simplest thing of all, a rubber cosh."

He fingered his bruise and gaped at her dazedly. "But it's mad! If you're thinking of a common burglary, there wasn't a thing in the place worth a man's while. Nobody'd be bothered burgling a cottage belonging to the likes of Bill and me, why should they? They always seem to know where the right stuff is. And if you mean something less accidental . . . if you're thinking I might have some sort of connection with crooks . . . I swear I haven't. I've never had anything to do with anybody like that. Not out of virtue, or anything, they just never came my way."

"You've got something there," she agreed. "The people who carry coshes are much the same sort of people who carry guns." She added pointedly: "Pippa had a gun.

You hadn't any acquaintance among the pros., but how do you know *she* hadn't?"

After a long moment of hurried calculation, swinging hurtfully between his anxiety to grasp at this life-line and his terror of finding it gossamer, he asked very quietly, his eyes clinging desperately to her face: "Bunty . . . do you really believe what you're saying? You wouldn't try to . . . soothe me, would you? Just out of kindness?"

"No," she said sturdily, "I wouldn't. I'm only saying what I mean."

"Then . . . what *do* you think happened?"

"I think someone else walked into that room—and I'll back my judgment by betting you what you like that you had your back to the door and Pippa was facing it—laid you out economically with a knock on the head, and then dealt with Pippa. For some reason of his own, which we don't know. As evidence for her having got involved in something in which she was out of her depth, there's the gun. As you say, what would such a girl as Pippa want with a gun? Where would she get one? It's the pros. and the would-be pros. who carry them. So there was Pippa dead, and you beautifully set up to take the blame. So beautifully that you yourself believed you'd killed her. That's the lines on which I'm thinking at this moment. But as yet we've hardly begun."

"Then in any case it looks as if I've cut my own throat, doesn't it?" he said with a lopsided grin. "I've run out and pointed the finger at myself. What do I do now? Who's ever going to believe I can possibly be innocent?"

"They might," said Bunty. "*I* believe it."

"Ah, *you*!"

She saw it in his eyes then, though she was too intent on the matter in hand to pay much attention, that for him she had become a creature immeasurably marvellous and unforeseen. But he didn't expect to find more than one of her.

"Bunty, what am I to do now? Go to the police and give myself up?"

"No," said the law-abiding police wife without hesitation. "Not yet! I've burned my boats, too, remember? I bought a few hours for consideration by lying to the police and sending them away. I gave a false name. To them I'm an accessory after the fact. What we do now is make use of the short time we've got in hand. Before we go to the police, let's see exactly what we have got, and have a go at making sense of it. The more evidence we can hand to them, the better prospects we've got."

"We?" he said softly, and one black eyebrow went up unexpectedly in sympathy with the corner of his mouth. A slightly wry, slightly careworn smile, but nevertheless a smile, the first she had seen on this haggard face.

"*We*!" she repeated with emphasis. "And the very first thing *you* do is get a few hours' sleep . . . and a bath, if it'll help. You've had no sleep for two nights, and I haven't had much, and we're going to need our wits about us. I'll tidy up this mess, and then I'll snatch a sleep, too."

"A bath!" His face brightened childishly. "I never thought I should be looking forward to anything again!"

"Go and get it, then. You'll be more use when you've had a rest, and can think straight again."

He rose and made for the door like a bidden child, dropping with sleep, but in the doorway he turned once again to look at her long and earnestly. His eyes had cleared into a pure, tired greyness, young and vulnerable and still heavy with trouble, but hesitant now on the edge of hope.

"Bunty. . . ."

She was already gathering up the scattered dishes from the tea-stained cloth, and piling them on the tray. She looked up at him inquiringly across the table.

" . . . what's the Bunty short for?"

She smiled. "Bernarda. But I don't tell everybody that. They took to calling me Bunny, and I wasn't having that, cuddly was the last thing I intended to be. So I twisted it into Bunty myself. At least that's got one sharp angle to it. What can I call you?"

"Luke. My name's Luke Tennant. *All* sharp angles. Bunty . . . Bernarda . . ." His voice touched the names with timid delicacy, like stepping-stones to what he wanted to say. "*I'm sorry!*" he blurted painfully. "Did I . . . hurt you very much. . . ?"

"No!" she said quickly. "Hardly at all. It's all right!" She had scarcely noticed the stiffness and soreness of her throat, and touched the bruises now with surprise.

"I'm sorry! How could I? I must have been clean out of my mind. . . ."

"Think nothing of it!" Bunty was beginning to experience a lightheadedness that could all too easily be mistaken for lightness of heart. She looked ruefully at the long scratch on his neck, on which a few beads of dried blood stood darkly. "I'm sorry I tried to kill you, too, for that matter. Neither of us was much good at it. Let's just say we both failed our practical, and call it quits!"

::   ::

The turmoil of hope had finally overwhelmed and wrecked him. He rolled himself in the quilt on the Alports' bed, and drowned in the vast sea of sleep that had been waiting for his first unguarded moment. And Bunty, having restored order in the living-room, lay down on the cushions of the settee and tried to think. It was the first time she had had a moment for thinking since this fantastic affair began, and it was the last such moment she would have until this affair ended. At least she was sure now of herself and him. But who could be sure of the ending?

She had meant to go carefully over his story, to try to extract from his halting account some significant point which had meant nothing to him. But as soon as she closed her eyes George's thin, middle-aged, scrupulous face was there within her eyelids, and she could see nothing else. If she had wanted something of her own to do, as proof that she had been in the world in her own right, she had it now, and for her soul's sake she must succeed in it; and George was far away and knew nothing about it, and could not help her. Be careful what you pray for, she thought wryly, you may get it. And to the beloved face within her closed eyes she said: You concentrate on your own case, chum, this one's mine—whether I like it or not. I got myself into it, and now I've got to get two of us out of it. You know how it is, there's no other way home. So go away, like a good boy, and let me think.

But he wouldn't go away; and in a few moments she let go of her anxieties and embraced the thought of him instead, with a still and grateful passion, and the instant she let her mind lie at rest in him she fell asleep.

It was nearly noon when she awoke, the sun was high, the light harder, more than half the room now out of the direct sunlight. She got up stiffly, sticky with sleep, and the sense of time pressing fell upon her like fear. She washed and made up her face, and then went to explore the contents of the kitchen cupboard. A canned Sunday luncheon was something of which her family would have disapproved, but it was better than nothing. There were no potatoes, of course, but there was rice, and ham, and some exotic canned vegetables. And blessedly, there was coffee. The kitchen was tiny, built out to the extremity of the level ground, with a broom-cupboard and a store under the same roof. She opened the back door, and the shimmering reflected light from the sea flooded in; and beyond a tiny, flagged terrace, the slatey stairs began to plunge downhill towards the inlet and the jetty, and the moored boat below.

She knew then, busy in the sunlit kitchen with can-opener and pans, that the silence and the brightness were an illusion, and nothing was going to be easily salvaged, neither Luke Tennant's liberty nor her own peace of mind.

::   ::

He came down the stairs with a brisk, self-conscious tread that told her plainly he meant to resume responsibility for his own fate. He was a new if slightly battered

man, polished, shaven, combed into aggressive neatness; he
was the lucky one in one respect, at least, he had his luggage with him on this trip. He had even changed his
clothes, perhaps as a symbolical gesture of hope and renewal. The sleep he had had, too short and too drunkenly
deep, had left him a little sick and unsteady, but very determined. His face was still pale, but the terrible tension was
eased once and for all. He could even smile properly. He
smiled when he opened the door of the living-room, and
looked for Bunty, and found her. It was as if his eyes had
been waiting with the smile in readiness, and she was the
spark that set light to it.

"I hope you're hungry," she said, rising. "You've probably got to be, to eat this concoction I've knocked up. It
was the best I could do. If you don't mind, I'll dish it up in
the kitchen and bring it in on the plates."

"Bunty, I've been . . ." His eyes took in the order she
had restored to the room, the laid table, the signs of activity
in the kitchen; he was side-tracked by sheer amazement,
and then abashed by a devastating sense of his own use-
lessness by comparison. "Good lord, you can't have slept
at *all*!"

"Oh, yes, I did," she called back from the kitchen.
"This is one of those five-minute meals. The only thing
that isn't instant, I'm glad to say, is the coffee." She
appeared in the kitchen doorway with the piled plates in
her hands, and closed the door behind her with one foot.
"Look out, these are hot!"

She had found Louise Alport's hostess apron, gaily
printed crash linen with pockets shaped like tulips, and her
nursery towelling oven gloves. The cottage had a fantasy
quality, unreal, inexhaustible, and in such dreamlike ex-
periences you take anything you can get, to balance the
everything you have lost, your normal world. Also, perhaps, for a better reason, to dazzle your companion, and
keep the machinery of his life ticking over until the normal
world is recovered.

If, of course, it ever is recovered.

"Bunty, I've been thinking . . ."

"Good!" she said heartily. "Maybe you can infect me. After lunch we've got a lot of hard thinking to do."

"Not we," he said gently. "*I.*"

She looked up sharply at that, eyeing him doubtfully across the table. He had regained his balance, at least; whether he yet believed seriously in his own innocence or not, he wasn't going to be shaken into induced behaviour again. No more doing his worst to act like a killer because he believed that he had reduced himself to that role, and had no right to any other.

"Bunty, I'm more grateful to you than I can ever tell you. But now I've got to go on with this by myself. It's my problem, not yours. I've let you do too much for me, and without you I should never have come to my senses. But now I *am* in my right mind, and I want you out of this mess, clean out of it. I want you home, untouched, as if you'd never known anything about me and my sordid affairs. After lunch I'm going to drive you into Forfar, and put you on a train for Edinburgh, on the way home. I'd make it all the way to Edinburgh, and see you safe on the express, only I doubt if I could get the car that far without being picked up."

"I doubt," said Bunty, laying down her fork with careful quietness, "whether you'll get it as far as Forfar, either."

"I think I shall. I know these roads. And you know what they said . . . they're looking for a car that jumped a red light and scared a policeman out of a year's growth, but not for a murderer. So they'll be hunting me, all right, but they won't have turned out the whole force after me. I'll make it safely to Forfar with you. And I shall feel a little less guilty if I know you're clear away. I can't let you go on carrying my load for me."

"Aren't you forgetting," she said dryly, "that they know I'm here? That I gave them a false name and address, which they may very well be checking up on at this moment? You think that young constable won't know me again?"

His eyes, devouring her with an unwavering stare of anxiety, compunction and reverence, said clearly that any man who had talked with her even for a moment would know her again among thousands. His voice, quietly reasonable, said only: " What does that matter? He's never going to see you again. All they've got is a false name. They may find out that your Rosamund doesn't exist, but that still won't help them to find Bunty. By tomorrow you'll be home again, and nobody'll know where you've been, and nobody here will know who the woman was who answered the door to the police this morning."

" It's impossible," said Bunty firmly. " In any case, I've got no money, not a penny."

" *We* have," he said, and smiled at her.

What surprised her most was the violence of the temptation that tugged at her mind and heart, to accept the offer and escape now, back into her old prosaic life, to close this secret interlude and lock the door on it for ever. She thought with an astonishing surge of joy and longing of her unexciting household in Comerford, and the half of her life that was over seemed to her in retrospect, and from this pinnacle of strangeness, full, satisfying and utterly desirable. Luke was not talking of impossibilities at all. By morning she could be home. No one would ever know where she'd been in the interval. Probably no one need ever know she had been away at all. *Not even George* !

The very mention, the very thought of George turned her in her tracks, and brought everything into focus for her. Of course she couldn't consider it. She had never seriously believed that she could.

"And what," she asked deliberately, " are *you* proposing to do?"

"As soon as I've seen you safely out of here I'm going to tidy up this place and leave it as nearly as possible the way we found it. Maybe I shan't succeed, but at least I can try to keep the Alports out of the deal. And then I'm going to take the car and everything that's in it, and somehow get myself to a police station without being picked up on the way. I can manage that much, if I put my mind to it. And I'll tell them everything I know about how Pippa got killed. Everything," he said, his grey gaze wide and steady on her face, " except about you. And then it will be up to them."

And I will remember you for ever, the grey eyes said, but not for her to hear; whether I ever see you again or not, and whatever becomes of me.

The moment of silence between them was brief and hypnotic; she couldn't let it go on, there were those urgent realities all the while drumming in her brain, and she knew, and it was time he knew, too, that she had no intention of going anywhere.

"Eat your lunch," she said practically, " it'll be even more revolting cold. You're wasting your time, in any case. I won't leave you. We're in this together, and we stand or fall together. I'm not going home to Comerbourne until I can take you with me, a free man."

In a sudden harsh gasp he burst out : " I meant to kill you !" and shuddered at the memory.

"I know you did. I know you meant to, but you couldn't. There was never any possibility that you'd be able to do it, when it came to the point. And neither can I go away and leave you now. Maybe I *meant to*, for a moment, but I can't. We mean to do things, out of some misconception of what we are, but what we really are always goes its own way when it comes to the point."

"I owe you everything I've got in the world now," he said carefully, " and everything I am, for whatever it's worth. You don't owe me anything, except a great deal of fear and pain." But he didn't say that he wanted her to go; it wouldn't have been true.

"That isn't how I see it. You chose me for a companion

in your extremity. But it happened to be my extremity, too, and I chose to accept your companionship for my own salvation. That's a bond, and I'm not going back on it. You didn't make it alone, I helped to make it. *We* made it," she said, "and now *we*'ve got to resolve it." And abruptly she rose from the table, and marched away into the kitchen for the coffee.

When she came back, he was staring out of the window with his chin on his fist, his face turned away from her; and she would never know whether he abandoned argument because he knew it would not be effective, or because he was only too afraid that it might, and he didn't want to lose her. For what he said, after a long pause, was only:

" Then I'd better bring in her things from the car, and see if there's anything there that means anything, to begin with."

" We should have a look at the gun, too," Bunty agreed, relieved.

" I suppose," he said, " I ought to bring *her* in, too." Bunty, watching his profile narrowly, noting its determined calm, and impersonality brittle as glass, saw sweat break in beads on his lip. " In any case I shall have to, to get at her suitcase."

She almost offered to help him, and realised in time that she must not. Where death was concerned she was stronger and better rehearsed than he was—hadn't she, in a sense, passed clean through a death of her own to this uncanny understanding of him? But there were now almost more ways of hurting and affronting him than there were of helping him, and most of them had to do with his wish to protect and spare her. She knew him now as well as she knew her own son, she was sensitive to everything that happened within him. It wouldn't cost her much to humour him. So she refrained from offering him the obvious comfort that would have shocked him deeply; for she had been on the point of reassuring him that by this

time rigor mortis would most probably be passing, and he
wouldn't have to struggle with a twisted marble girl.

::   ::

He laid her down carefully on the bed, and turned back
the folds of the blanket from her. She was limp and pliant
in his hands. He settled her head on the pillow, and
straightened her legs and arms, trying to remember whether
there had been any expression of fear in her face, where
now there was nothing but indifference, and sadly conscious that he would have been unable to see it for the fear
in himself. The dead never look as if they are alive and
sleeping, whatever people may say. They always look dead.
There is an absolute quality about death.

So there she was, young and slender and lovely, the sum
of three years of his life, and the focal point of everything
he knew about suffering. And maybe he had killed her,
but in his heart he felt an increasing conviction that he
had not. If he could have been quite sure of his innocence
he might have felt the last convulsion of love for her at
this moment; but because he was not quite sure, all he
dared feel was a terrible, aching pity at such cruel waste.
He smoothed her long, fair hair on either side of her face,
trying to make something orderly out of disorder.

Then he locked the door, and went down to bring in her
suitcase and handbag from the car.

CHAPTER VII

THE GUN LAY between them on the table, a tiny, compact
shape of bluish steel, hardly more than four inches long, to
the outward view of so simple and innocent a construction
that it looked more like a theatrical property or a toy than
a machine for killing. It had a tiny cameo head engraved
on the side of the grip, and the lettering along the barrel
clearly announced its name and status:

LILIPUT KAL. 6.35
Modell 1925.

" I suppose there's no point in handling it carefully," said
Bunty, eyeing it dubiously. " We've already plastered the
outside of it with our prints, and in any case we can be
certain they haven't left any others there to be found."

Nevertheless, neither of them was in any hurry to touch
it again. This trifle, hardly too big to have fallen out of a
child's lucky-bag, had bound them together and held them
rigidly apart the whole night long, but it had no place in
their relationship now. For a moment Bunty had an impulse to ask him why, when he had dragged himself to
the very brink of murder against his nature, he had not,
after all, used the gun. But that was only one of the many
things she could never ask him, and in any case he would
not have known the answer. On reflection, she felt that
she might be better able to explain it to him. The Luke
who had approached that moment in such sickness and
despair had believed himself—no, had *known* himself—to
be a murderer; but his own blood and sinews had felt no
conviction of any such identity, and had done everything
possible to avoid making it true. The gun might have made
success only too certain, and his hands had shirked it at the
last moment, and come to the decision naked, and still
fighting hard against what he was trying to make them
do. So she was alive, and he . . .

He picked up the Liliput suddenly, and thumbed over
the small, grooved catch at the left side of the grip. " It's all
right," he said, holding it out to her with a faint smile,
" I've only put it on safety. That won't foul up any
evidence there may be, and if we're going to handle it we
may as well take no chances." He caught the sudden
kindling flare of her eyes, and made haste to answer before
she asked. " No, really, it hasn't been like that all the
time. I put the safety on after I came round, as soon as I
made up my mind I had to get out and take everything

with me. I don't even know why. I suppose I was afraid
to handle it without, not being used to such things. Pippa
was no good with it, either," he said wryly, "she had to
shove it over with her free hand instead of just using her
thumb. She always had to wrestle with anything manual,
even bottle-openers."

Bunty turned the little thing incredulously in her hand.
It couldn't have weighed much more than half a pound.
"You mean it was on safety all that time. . . ." She let it
go there, sparing a brief smile for the memory of her
night's ordeal. His subconscious rebellion against death
had certainly been doing its best for him and for her.

"I think so. I *hope* so! I don't actually know which
way is which, and I haven't fired it, to find out. But you
can't help picking up the general principles if you see
enough telly serials. And she certainly wasn't in any mood
to be switching it on to safety when she started waving it at
me. And it wasn't muzzled when it killed her, either, that's
for sure. I only pushed the catch off again," he said,
paling, "when the police . . . when you went to the
door. . . ."

She knew exactly when he must have given this little
snake its teeth back, and for what purpose, and the less he
thought about that now, the better. "I suppose we can
take it for granted," she said briskly, "that this *is* the gun
that killed her? It's the only way it makes sense. They
wouldn't leave you there holding a different one, what
would be the use? As soon as the police had recovered the
bullet you'd have been in the clear. We could at least have
a look how many shots have been fired from it, couldn't
we? How do you open this thing, do you know?"

He took it from her. "Most of them seem to have a
little catch at the bottom of the butt, and the magazine
slots in there. This must be it . . . " His finger was on the
little clip when she suddenly caught him by the wrist, her
eyes flaring.

"No, wait . . . don't! I've just thought of something! What's it like, this magazine thing?"

"A sort of little oblong steel box with one side open. You slot the bullets in, and a spring moves them up singly into the chamber. I *think*! But we can have a look," he said reasonably.

"No, don't open it! If there are good hard surfaces, like that, it would hold prints, wouldn't it? Whoever loaded it would have to handle it . . . and I know we've completely wrecked any chances there might have been of getting anything off the outside, and in any case there wouldn't be any traces there but ours. But we haven't touched the inside! And I bet nobody thought of wiping that part off before they planted it on you."

"But it isn't going to tell us anything, is it?" he objected ruefully. "Whoever shot Pippa didn't have to touch the magazine. *She* was the one who loaded it. . . ."

"Ah, but *was* she? How do we know that? She got that gun from somebody else, probably somebody shady. And you said yourself, she was hopeless with her hands, she had to wrestle with things. If she got somebody to give her a gun, *wouldn't she get him to load it for her, too*?"

"You could be right, at that!" he agreed, reflecting the cautious glow of her excitement back to her; and he took his finger from the clip in haste. "You don't think, do you, that the chap who gave it to her may be the same as the chap who killed her?"

"Why not? Pippa got into something that was too deep for her, if you ask me, and where the guns are the motives for murder often are, too. But even if we only find out who gave it to her, that'll be something. You know," said Bunty intently, "what really puzzles me about Pippa? Not so much why she dropped you—most likely that was when she picked up with this other man—but why she picked you up again. Not out of any affection, you soon found that out. She wasn't changing back, not on the level. No, she came running after you and made herself charming again because she wanted something out of you."

"It would make sense," he agreed painfully, remembering Pippa alive, ambitious and energetic. "Only she never actually asked me for much, did she? A trip to London in my company. Oh, yes, and the loan of the car on Thursday, because she was going shopping for clothes. It's a bind, getting on buses with dress-boxes. She brought it back in the evening, and we went to a cinema. But that's all she asked from me. And what is there in that?"

"But that drive to London with you she wanted very, very badly. She showed you that when you held out on her. What could possibly have been so urgent about it? I mean, she could as easily have got herself there by train, if she wanted to go as badly as all that. But that wouldn't do. *It had to be with you.*"

"But why? Why should it matter to her how she ran out, even if for some reason she had to run?"

"I don't know. But Pippa knew. She knew of a very strong reason indeed, or why should she still go on persisting, even when she found out that you knew about her visitor, and weren't going to be taken in any more? When she couldn't get her own way by charm, she was even desperate enough to use the gun. And now I've thought of something else about this gun. You were meant to be found right there on the spot, a sitting duck, ready to be charged. Either still out, or half-dizzy and half-drunk, dithering over the body and not knowing which way to run. Caught red-handed with a murder you couldn't even begin to deny . . . even believing yourself guilty. . . ."

"Yes," he said, "that's the way it would have been."

"Then," she said, closing her eyes tightly in concentration, "whoever planted you would have to take steps to ensure that you *should* be found like that. He *couldn't* leave it to chance. I'd stake my life that the police got an anonymous telephone call to go to your house, just as soon as the other fellow had made sure he was out of range.

From a public call box. Not too near. He'd have liked to keep a watch and make sure everything went according to plan, but he wouldn't risk it. Professionals don't take chances, he'd get well away. And you said you were only out about twenty-five minutes. . . . Whoever he was, he was relying on having much longer than that."

She opened her eyes, wide, brilliant, greenish-hazel, and stared at him. " You know what? I reckon you slid from under simply by having a good hard head, and coming round more quickly than anyone could have expected. Your part was to be discovered groggy and helpless with drink, if not still out, with the girl dead on the floor and the gun still in your hand, caught in the very act. Instead, you came round too early and scared sober, cleaned up the place, ran for the car, and got out with all the evidence. And you know, I begin to think it may have been the best thing you could do."

" Maybe I had one more small stroke of luck," he said, taking fire almost reluctantly from her sparks. " I'm sure about one thing, we were wrestling for the gun, and somehow we lost our balance and started to fall. Supposing someone coming in behind me had just let loose with a cosh—just *supposing* it's true—then if I was already falling with the blow I should partially ride it. And he might not even know."

" And that *is* how you were placed? I was right? You had your back to the door?"

" More or less, yes. If you'd known Pippa . . . She owned whatever she made part of her outfit, like me. She owned whatever was mine. When she walked in, she walked right in. You always ended up with your back to the door."

" So if either of you saw a third person enter, it would be Pippa. Did her face change? Did she cry out?"

" Oh, God, do I know?" he said, groaning with the effort to remember clearly. " We were so tangled, neither of us knew about anyone else but the two of us. I don't

know. . . . I don't remember. . . . She was yelling at me
all the time, what would one yell more mean?"

"No, I see that. No, don't worry, it wouldn't prove anything, anyhow. Let it go."

"Bunty," he said suddenly, reaching across the table to
touch her hand, "I don't want you to hope too much, and
find yourself badly let down in the end. God knows you've
made me begin to believe I couldn't have done it, but
everything we've got is only conjecture. There isn't one
blind bit of evidence to show that there was ever anyone
else there but the two of us. Not one! Not that I'm giving
up so easily, I don't mean that . . . I don't *want* to believe
I'm a killer. But if it should turn out . . . I don't want *you*
hurt!" he concluded with abrupt passion, and plucked
his hand away.

There could hardly, Bunty thought, be a better demon-
stration of her contention that he had nothing of the killer
about him, and not even his own despairing conviction had
been able to instil the makings into his nature. Here was
he struggling to extend himself to accept the possibility of
his guilt, and his chief worry was to save her from becoming so involved that she might be seriously damaged by the
disillusionment.

"Give me time," she said, wisely sticking to the practical point he had raised, "and I'll find the sign you want.
I'll *prove* there was someone else there. There wasn't, for
instance, anything missing from the body? Or from the
house?"

He shook his head with a wry smile. "That's just what
I was thinking of, as a matter of fact. Pippa's still wearing
her engagement ring! It isn't such a valuable job, I know,
but surely if some sort of crook acquaintance had followed
her to my place and killed her, he'd have gone to the trouble
to take a solitaire diamond from her finger before he left?
It wouldn't delay him long."

She thought that over rapidly, her lip caught in her
teeth. "That could also mean something that seems to me

much more likely. After all, you don't just kill over a slight difference of opinion, or a few shillings in crooked money. The mere fact that it was worth murder suggests to me that whoever it was wasn't interested in one ring, not even on the side. What was at stake was bigger than that. The ring was worth more to him right there on Pippa's finger when the police came, to make them say just what you're saying: If there'd been an intruder here, he'd have made off with this. Everything *had* to be left intact, or there was a hole in the case against you."

"Then how," he asked with a perverse smile, "are you ever going to produce that sign for me?"

"You want to bet?" said Bunty. "Don't side-track me, and we'll get there yet. Where were we? Yes . . . with you set up as the fall guy, and the murderer telephoning the police from a suitably distant call box. Now you can take it as read that the police would *have* to check on such a call, whether they took it seriously or not, simply because it always *might* be true. In this case they found only an empty house, locked and innocent, no body, no criminal, no gun, nothing—just a bachelor cottage with the two tenants gone off for their half-term breaks, as probably some neighbour would confirm. Or the school caretaker, if there isn't a neighbour who occasionally swops gossip with you. All in order. So what would they do next? Shrug it off as a false alarm? They *do* happen, all too often, out of spite, or boredom, or just a perverted sense of humour. Or would they put in the squad and go over the place thoroughly? In their present state, shorthanded and overworked, and taking into account the surface improbability of two respectable young men like you getting involved in murder, I'd say they wouldn't spare the time. On the other hand, they'd still be a little bit curious, just as to what was behind that call."

"Do you think the caller would mention names?" Luke asked alertly.

"A good point! No, I don't think he would. The

more anonymous your anonymous call is, so to speak, the less likely ever to tie up with you. No, he wouldn't mention Pippa's name, certainly not if he had some traceable connection with her himself. He'd just say, you boys want to get along to such-and-such an address, fast, there's a girl been killed in there."

"Then when the police drew a blank at my place, they'd have no way of following up by checking on Pippa's flat and movements. So what more *could* they do?"

"I'll tell you. They could pass out to the papers a little news item about the police being called to an apparently false alarm of the murder of a girl at a Comerbourne address. And then they'd sit back and wait to see if somebody comes forward with word of a daughter, or a sister, or a friend, going missing. No details, of course, just the general bait."

"But to-day," he said, "is Sunday."

"Exactly. And the Sunday papers go to press before Saturday evening, and couldn't even get this para. into the stop-press. So nothing can result until at least to-morrow. For my money, the police don't yet know, *nobody* yet knows but you and I and the murderer, that Pippa is dead. Which matches with what the police here said. All they were following up was a case of dangerous driving."

"That does give us a little time, anyhow," he acknowledged.

"And a hypothetical good mark if we're the ones who come forward voluntarily to report her death and tell all we know about it."

He had turned away to pick up Pippa's suitcase, but he swung on his heel then to take a long, considering look at her. Her face was intent, candid and utterly serious.

"You really have a lot of faith in the police, haven't you?" he said, studying her curiously.

"Yes. They're human, and not all of them what they ought to be, but by and large, yes, I've got a lot of faith in them. Bring that over here on the settee, where the light's good."

Pippa Gallier's suitcase was of the air-travel persuasion, large but light, in oatmeal-coloured fibreglass with a rigid frame, and secured, in addition to its twin locks, with a broad external strap. Luke laid it on the couch, unbuckled the strap, and tried one of the locks with his thumb. The flap sprang back at once, a success he had not expected. He released the other one, and opened the case on as tempting a collection of feminine fashion as Bunty had ever seen under one lid. Pippa had loved clothes, and cared for them tenderly. Everything was delicately folded and cunningly assembled, protected in plastic and held in place by pink corded ribbon. Luke shrank from touching these relics, almost as much from awe of their perfection as from re-membrance of their owner. It was Bunty who loosed the ribbon tethers, and began to lift out the upper layers carefully, surveying each before she removed it.

" She did herself well. Doesn't it seem to you that a lot of this is brand-new?"

" I told you, she took the car shopping on Thursday. I said she'd have time to shop in London, but she couldn't wait. She loved clothes," he said helplessly, watching delicate feminine colours lifted one by one from Pippa's treasury.

" I see she did. Too well," said Bunty sharply, " to have let *this* pass when she was packing."

He had noticed nothing wrong, and indeed there was little to notice, just a corner of a folded skirt in its plastic envelope crumpled together like a buckled wing after a collision, stubbed into creases. And directly below that, the lace edge of a slip folded back on itself. Bunty slid her hand into the corner and felt down past layer after layer, turning them back to examine each as she came to it. Then she readjusted them, a glint of excitement in her eye, and treated all the other corners in the same way.

" You see?"

He didn't see; his own packing would have looked so different that this still appeared perfection, but it is on perfection that tiny blemishes show most clearly.

"He was very neat, he hardly disturbed anything, but he left his traces, all the same. She'd never have left those corners crumpled like that, not even by one fold. Even if she had to disturb her case again to put in something else, she'd do the job properly. Somebody has been through this case, hunting for something. Something big enough to be easily found, because he didn't lift out the things, he just ran his hands down in the corners and here, at the front, and felt for it. And what's more," she said with certainty, "*he didn't find it*!"

"Oh, now, hold it! How can you possibly know that?"

"Because if he had, something big enough to be located that way, he would have to lift things out to get at it, or else pull it out by force from under, and in either case we'd be able to tell. If anything sizable had been yanked from under these pretties, not only would they have been disarranged a good deal more, but also the hole where the thing had been would be there to be seen and felt. You try it, some time. And even if he'd lifted things out, I think I'd be able to tell the difference. Besides, I doubt if he had time."

"He certainly didn't have too much, but . . ." He was afraid to believe too readily in her conclusions. She might consider this as proof positive that some third person had been present in the cottage that night, but he was still waiting for the unmistakable sign, something that didn't depend on opinion, something as positive as a fingerprint.

"I wonder," said Bunty, "what he was looking for?" She closed the lid again over the delicate remains of Pippa's human vanity, and turned to their last card, the large handbag of cream-coloured glove-leather, soft as velvet and almost as expensive as mink. "This is new, too? She was really intending to start afresh, wasn't she?"

He said sombrely: "Yes"; thinking, but not with me.

Bunty unclasped the opulent bag, and turned it upside-down over the table, letting its contents slide out gently through her fingers to be spread out on the polished surface and examined almost in one glance. She moved the items aside one by one, innocuous things like comb, handkerchief, purse-cum-wallet, stamp-case, compact, lipstick, tissues in a clear plastic holder, Quickies . . .

" . . . ball-pen, manicure, Kwells. . . . Was she a bad traveller in a car?"

"Not that I know of. But we hadn't made any long trips together before. Maybe she was. When you come down to it, I didn't really know much about her."

" . . . a folder about what's on in London, a small wallet of hair-grips. That's all. Well?"

"Well?" he repeated, without understanding. "Yes, that's all. Nothing remarkable there." His voice was discouraged, though he tried to keep it level and reasonable. What, after all, had he been expecting? "Nothing there to tell us anything new."

"Oh, no?" said Bunty. "*Then where are her keys?*"

::   ::

"Keys?" he echoed, shaken, blinded, transfigured with realisation. "*Keys!*"

He began to shake uncontrollably, and she put her arm round him and held him strongly, watching his face. In similar circumstances she might even have ventured to put her arms round Dominic, yes, even at his ripe, daunting age of twenty, rising twenty-one, though with Dominic she would have had to go very much more carefully, simply because he was her son, and still a little in love with her, and terribly in love with someone else, and jealous of his own manhood. Luke was an easier case, their relationship, complex as it might be, had not that ultimate complexity.

"Yes, her keys. Didn't you think of them? Her suitcase wasn't locked, was it? Would Pippa go anywhere with her suitcase unlocked? Of course she locked it! Of course she had her keys with her, here, in this handbag. She was locking up her flat, wasn't she? She was locking her luggage. He—whoever he was—he took her keys to look through her case, and he didn't find what he was looking for, so he kept the keys. Why? To look for it in her flat . . . don't you think so?"

She led him in her arm to the nearest of the white wicker chairs and persuaded him into it, and sat on the arm and held him against her shoulder, talking to him in a soft, reasonable, detached voice, coaxing and reassuring without directly doing either.

"He wanted something she had, or something he believed she had. He thought it would be in her case, but it wasn't. So he went to her flat to hunt for it there. Now you know," she said, and had no need, and felt none, to explain what it was that he knew.

"There *was* someone there," he said, suddenly laughing, shaking with laughter like a lunatic. "I *didn't* . . ." And he put his head down in her lap and laughed and wept, with relief, with rapture, because he wasn't a murderer.

::   ::

"She always carried them," he said, clearly, almost gaily, staring out over a sea now deep-blue and shadow-green in the late afternoon light. His face was warm, human, mobile, with fluctuating colour and live, ardent eyes. His age, which went up and down on the yo-yo of circumstances, had steadied at twenty-seven, and now he was well able to hold it there. "She was a person who took care to lock things. She had a little leather case shaped like a climbing boot, she'd bought it somewhere in the Tyrol, one holiday. A little kid climbing boot with a key-ring. You fitted your keys on the ring, and it went inside the boot, and the boot zipped up. She wouldn't go away without that! And it isn't here. And I didn't take it. So somebody else did. So I believe—I *believe* now!—that I didn't kill her. Someone *did* come in on us. I *was* set up purposely to take the blame. Can you credit it?" he said, lost in wonder. "Now I don't even care so much if they convict me. Just so I know I didn't do it."

"They're not going to convict you," said Bunty quietly. She had taken her arm from him, even withdrawn herself from the arm of the chair and left him unsupported, as soon as he reared himself up intact and joyful, with that fresh, live face she had never seen before, but which she liked on first sight. "They can reason, too. And they'll listen, I'll see to that. And there's her flat in Comerbourne, that ought to furnish some evidence, too. The gun . . . her suitcase searched . . . her keys missing . . . We've got something to offer, now."

He looked at the light, and he looked at the poor little relics disposed about the table. Then he looked again over the sea, and calculated chances, and wondered.

"Maybe we ought to wait a little, just until it's dusk? I should hate to be picked up now. I want to drive up to the police station and report in without any question of compulsion."

"We could wait a little longer," said Bunty. "Why don't you put the boat away, while we're waiting?"

He had forgotten about the boat, riding gently beside the jetty, nuzzling its fenders like a kitten as the water rocked under it. It must be nearly full tide now, the deck swaying high, and the inlet full to its limit. It seemed a life-time since he had hoisted those two stones aboard, and covered them guiltily from sight. He could hardly believe, now, in the person he had been during those morning hours, so short a time ago. Bunty had peeled that incubus off from his flesh and spirit, and brought him to this in-toxicating freedom, which was proof against any charge others might bring.

He looked at her across the white and orange room, and tried to assess the quality she had for him, and the physical aspects of her that expressed, so inadequately, her essence. So beautiful, with that chestnut hair like a ripe brown cap moving suavely round her head, and those few grey strands so alive and silvery that they set light to every movement she made, like attendant spirits embracing and guarding her. Powdered freckles golden over the bridge of a straight nose. And those eyes for which his experience had no measure, so blazingly honest and gallant and clear, at once green and golden and brown, the eyes that had first drawn him to her. They were looking at him now with a direct, contented regard in which he found undoubted affection, but did not dare find more.

But I love you, he thought, I shall love you for ever and ever and ever, as long as I live, and with everything there is left of me that knows how to love, even after I'm dead. I had no conception that there could be a kind of love like this, or a kind of person like you. Utterly without deceit, or meanness, or the very shadow of anything second-rate. I thought one always had to compromise, to make allowances, to be ready to come to terms with love. Nobody ever told me you were possible, or I would never have settled for anything less.

"Yes, of course," he said, fumbling after ordinary words through the golden haze of a revelation for which no expression was possible, "I'd better get Reggie's treasure under cover."

And he took off his coat and slung it on the back of a chair, putting on instead an old duffle jacket that Reggie Alport left permanently hanging in the hall cupboard, as working gear for when the east coast proved blustery and unkind. In a few moments Bunty, putting away crockery and tools in the kitchen, heard his footsteps, unbelievably light and young now, leaping down the slatey stairs towards the water.

CHAPTER VIII

BY THE TIME Bunty had washed out the stained table-cloth and hung it to dry, and sat down to wait for Luke's return, she was no longer entirely easy in her mind about those keys. Supposing she had read too much into their absence, and built him up on insufficient evidence to another shattering fall? What if they were upstairs all the time, for instance, in Pippa's coat pocket? No, that was hard to believe. Someone who loved clothes so much wouldn't spoil the set of them by carrying things of any bulk or weight in the pockets. Which is why the handbags of to-day have grown bigger than shopping bags.

I don't know, though, thought Bunty on reflection. This year's coats have at least got flared skirts again, not straight, so that even a loose threepenny-bit shows through in a duodecagonal bump. Why not slip up and make sure, now, while Luke's out of the house?

He would have locked the bedroom, of course, she quite understood that. She was to be protected from touching or seeing again the sad wreckage of his first love. But there was his coat on the back of the chair by the desk, and there was a good chance that the key was in his pocket. He need never know that she had circumvented his concern for her feelings, if she made her search at once.

The bedroom key was there, she found it in the left-hand outside pocket. She ran up the stairs, and let herself into the pastel-coloured room; and there on the bed lay the youth and beauty for whose passing she had been startled into grieving only two days ago. Wasted and spoiled, and withdrawn now into supreme indifference, Pippa was never going to look into her mirror at forty-one, and wonder if everything had been well done, and whether this was all. Just being alive again would have been prize enough for Pippa. Bunty stood beside the bed and looked down at her with wonder and pity. Touching her started no other feelings, no repugnance at all; Bunty had seen death before.

The charcoal-coloured coat had fine silver threads running through the weave, a flared skirt, and two large slant pockets. There was nothing in them, but the trouble was that they were cut so wide and shallow that they might easily shed their contents when the wearer was recumbent. Better look in the boot of the car, too, and make quite sure. The matching skirt had no pockets. Slenderly cut for an almost hipless figure, it could not possibly have accommodated one. There was nowhere else to look. Bunty passed her hands all down the still, chill body, avoiding the encrusted brown hole in the fine cream sweater. No, Pippa had no keys. And no more use for keys.

The large, delicate eyelids, blue-veined like pale harebells, were imperfectly closed. A faint gleam of reflected light from the hooded eyes followed Bunty to the door. She looked back once, and the stillness of the slight figure had the quality of tomb sculpture, monumental not so much in the absence of movement as in the total renunciation of movement. The infection of silence and stealth that possesses the living in the presence of death is not awe but sympathetic magic, used as a protection. Do your best not to seem alien and alive here, and death won't recognise another victim and turn on you.

Bunty tiptoed out of the room, and closed and locked the door. She was still moving soundlessly when she slipped the bedroom key back into Luke's pocket. Poor girl! How old could she have been? Twenty-three or twenty-four? She didn't look so much, but apparently she was senior enough to be a deputy buyer at a first-class store like Pope Halsey's. Probably very good at her job; a pity, a thousand pities, she hadn't been content to stick to it, but had meddled with something out of her scope.

The garage key was hanging on its own proper hook in the kitchen; Luke had made no attempt to hide it, once he had brought Pippa and her belongings into the house. Bunty took it, let herself out by the front door, and crossed the gravel to the creosoted timber building, large enough for two cars. She unlocked the door and went in. There was the big old Rover, a hulking black shape in the light from the dusty window, unfashionable, powerful and solid, built when cars were meant to last, and to run remorselessly until every part dropped dead together. At the last moment she wondered if Luke would have locked the boot again, and whether she would have to go back and hunt for more keys; but the huge lid gave easily to her hand, and bounced open to its fullest. There was nothing to hide in there now.

Pippa had travelled a great many miles in this dark coffin, and there had been some pretty rough riding on the way. The Tyrolean climbing boot could very easily have rolled out of those shallow pockets and into a dark corner here, and escaped notice. But no, there was nothing to be found but a gallon can for petrol, the spare wheel braced to one side, and a wooden tool-box and a jack shoved well to the back. Bunty moved those items which were movable, and felt all round the dusty floor until she was satisfied. Nothing. And the thing could hardly have found its way into the petrol can or the tool box.

Nevertheless, for no good reason, she opened the lid of the box. A roughish affair, but solid, maybe as old as the car. There was a top tray full of small tools and a good deal of accumulated rubbish, of the kind one keeps because it may come in useful some day, and finally throws out in a grand clearance about two days before the occasion for its usefulness does arise. She lifted the tray. It sat upon two stout wooden supports, and below was a larger compartment.

The clean, new, flat package that lay there, almost as large as the inside dimensions of the box, and wrapped neatly in decorative bookshop paper, startled her by its sheer incongruity. It was about fifteen inches by ten, and could easily have been one of the lavish gift-books currently fashionable for leaving negligently around on coffee-tables. Only it wasn't. She prodded it, and it had no bound hardness, but a thick, yielding, heavy, papery quality. It might have been unremarkable enough almost anywhere else;

but here it arrested her attention like the eruption of a Roman candle.

She lifted it out, and on impulse pulled at the end of the pink tape that tied it, and unwrapped it at one end. It felt like paper, and it was paper. Neat bundles of thin, limp oblongs printed in sepia browns and muted greens on white, and held together in regular order by girdles of narrow brown gumstrip. Six bundles in one layer, four of them ranged side by side, and two lengthways alongside them; and several layers.

She riffled the ends through her fingers unbelievingly, and stared, and stared again. She had never seen so many ten-pound notes in her life. At a lightning estimate, she was holding in her hands something over twelve thousand pounds.

:: ::

For just one moment her mind recoiled with horror and revulsion, suddenly seeing a Luke who had been lying to her throughout, who had been in some shady deal with the girl, and killed her over the proceeds. Here was this bundle hidden in his tool box, in his car, and here was he on the coast, ready and equipped with a boat for his escape, and funds to keep him afloat wherever he went.

It shook her to the heart, but it was gone as suddenly as it had come. It blew through her mind like a gust of wind, and died into invulnerable calm. No, she had the best possible reason to know better than that. If he had killed Pippa, then Bunty Felse, too, would have been dead by now, there would have been no recoil from the act. He wasn't a killer, and he would be the least effective of partners in anything criminal. Moreover, her instinct told her that he could not possibly have been acting all this time. For what purpose, even if he had the ability? No, she had not really been shaken. She knew she was right about him. She would stake her life on it. She *was* staking her life on it.

Not Luke. Pippa.

Hadn't he mentioned twice that she had borrowed his car to carry home her shopping on Thursday?

So that was why she had been frantic when Luke had told her in no uncertain terms that they weren't going anywhere, when she had found him disillusioned, and the car still in the garage, and out of her reach for ever. She couldn't tell him about the money, and she couldn't get access to her hiding-place to recover it. She had put it clean out of her own reach. No wonder she raved, no wonder she committed the final folly and threatened him with the gun.

Yes, someone had been involved in crooked business, but it wasn't Luke. Pippa was running out in a hurry with hot money, but it wasn't from Luke she was running. On the contrary, she had run back to him and ingratiated herself with him afresh in order to make use of him for her get away. That was what she had wanted of him. That was what she had had in mind when she came back and couldn't have been sweeter. And his engagement ring? Well, a little bonus like that is always welcome. Why say no? He was more likely to do what she wanted if she accepted him. And a solitaire diamond, even a little one, is not to be sneezed at.

There were more and more implications crowding in beyond these. Bunty was dizzy with the flashing of chaotic particles falling into place, as though a jigsaw puzzle had abruptly decided to solve itself.

Any minute now Luke would be coming up from the sea. Let him find this parcel as she had found it, let him demonstrate to himself as well as to her what the find meant in terms of his own integrity. And let him destroy for ever, in the finding, whatever grain of doubt had remained to suggest to her, even for an instant, what she had just found herself momentarily believing. He had a right to know that she had doubted, provided he understood that the doubt was the last.

She smoothed the end of the package hastily back into

order, re-tied it exactly as before, and replaced it in the tool box. She closed the boot, locked the garage and went back to put the key in its place.

Presently Luke came up from the inlet, with the salt smell of the coast eddying from the shoulders of Reggie Alport's jacket. She let him hang it up in the hall cupboard, and put on his own coat again, before she leaned out from the kitchen and said: "You don't think she could have had her keys in her pocket, after all, do you?"

He shook his head emphatically. He had had that slight figure in his arms, and composed it into order on the bed, he knew there was nothing in her pockets. She wasn't a pocket girl, anyhow, she was an outsize-handbag girl.

"And they couldn't have slipped out while she was in the boot? I only want," she said, "to make *certain* that someone took them."

"I don't think so for a moment," said Luke, "but it won't take a minute to have a look." And he reached for the key of the garage, and led the way blithely.

::   ::

He found it. She didn't even have to prompt him. He groped all round with buoyant thoroughness in the huge boot, shoved the petrol can aside, scooped a hand round the spare wheel, and hoisted the lid of the tool box.

"Nothing," he said; and then, arrested by a capricious memory: "Do you know, this is the only thing I ever made in woodwork class at school? Not much finesse, but you must admit the zeal."

He was happy, he hoped for grace, and believed in justice, and he knew, *knew* he was not a murderer. She wondered how there could have remained to her even one scruple of insecurity. After all, few people in the world could know him as well as she now knew him; not even his mother, if he still had a mother, knew him better.

"A tour-de-force," she said. "What do you keep underneath, Black and Decker's total output? It's nearly big enough."

"Junk, mostly," he said. "I'm a jackdaw." And he hoisted the tray in one hand, himself fleetingly curious.

"Hey!" he said sharply, his voice losing its reminiscent ease. "What's this? I've never . . . Father Christmas has been!" But there was no recapturing the note of innocence. Wary, mystified and calm, he lifted out the book that was no book, and studied the gay wrapping paper, dotted with variegated bookworms of all ages, with their noses appropriately buried. "I don't understand. *I* didn't put this in here."

"What is it?" asked Bunty at his shoulder. "Open it!"

And he opened it, on the lid of the boot, sweeping the folds of paper aside with a large vigour which it seemed belonged to him when he was in possession of himself. She watched the sudden rigidity of his face, the dropped jaw, the bewildered eyes, the wonderfully quick apprehension. All genuine. What she was less prepared for was the instant understanding, the blazing intelligence with which he turned his face upon her.

"You knew, didn't you? You'd already found it?"

No bitterness, no accusation, only that quick, alert, brittle tone of someone who feels ice cracking under him. She had every right in the world to put him to the test; the ache in him was only the longing to be found intact after the test was over.

"Yes," she said, "I found it while you were down at the boat."

"I give you my word, I didn't know."

"I know you didn't. I wondered for about five seconds," she said steadily, "but that was all. No, Pippa put it there, of course. It was why she had to go to London with you. No other car would do. And it was why she died."

He had paled afresh at the revelation of how difficult and new and vulnerable was his relationship with her. You had to work at this as hard as at a marriage. What was more surprising was the clarity with which they both suddenly saw that there would never be any need for a second such assay. From that moment they knew each other through and through.

::   ::

They locked the garage again, and took their find into the house and there opened it upon the living-room table. All that money, they couldn't believe in it. Neither of them had ever seen so much.

"So *that*'s why she was in such a state when I told her to get out," said Luke, looking down at it with a shadowed face, almost afraid to touch. "And that's what *he* was looking for. He searched her case, and then took the keys away to search her flat, and all the time it was where she'd hidden it, in my car. Where do you suppose she got it?"

"It's stolen money. What other possibility is there? I can't believe she was up to anything on her own. Somebody deposited this with her until it cooled enough to be distributed or moved out of the area. And before the heat was off she'd had it in her possession so long she'd come to think of it as hers—so much in clothes and clubs and parties and travel and fun. Everything she wanted. She'd begun to question whether it ever need be distributed at all. Who could make better use of it than she could?"

"You really think it may be that? I know she was extravagant and spoiled . . . But she'd never . . . Oh, I don't know!" he said helplessly, winding the pink tape nervously round his fingers.

"What else could it be? How could she come by this much money in cash, otherwise? And if she had, honestly, why *keep* it in cash and have it hanging around? And why did she acquire a gun, unless it was because she had something to protect, and somebody willing and able to find her a gun to protect it with? Who carries this kind of money in a parcel? Not honest people." Bunty sat down and stared at the uncovered notes, brooding with her head in her hands. "How long has Pippa worked in Comerbourne?"

"Nearly three years. I met her soon after I started work there."

"Then this comes from some local coup," she said with authority, and closed her eyes the better to think back over recent history. The sight of all those miniature queens, so demure and complacent in whatever hands, was distracting. "You said she started getting off-hand with you about two months ago. That was probably when she first picked up with these people. And just over a week ago she came back and began to make up to you. And she worked at Pope Halsey's, as an assistant buyer. . . ."

Her voice snapped off abruptly. She opened her eyes wide, bright-green in this slanting pre-evening light, dazzled eyes. "Oh, no! That *must* be it! Tell me again, Luke, what department did she work in?"

"I don't think I did tell you. But it was furs," he said, puzzled, forgetting the money in her intensity. "Why?"

"And she was assistant to the buyer?"

"Yes . . . she used to model furs for their advertisements. She looked marvellous . . . I've seen the stills. . . ." He caught Bunty's bright stare, fixed as a fortune-teller's crystal-hypnotised gaze, and trembled with a premonition of final truth. "*Why?*"

"There was a big van-load of furs," she said like a clairvoyant, "coming from London for Pope Halsey, just about six weeks ago. It was hi-jacked soon after it left the M.1, flagged down near a lay-by, by somebody pretending there'd been an accident. The driver was picked up with bad concussion next day, the van was ditched on a minor road. The furs were gone, clean trade. Probably turned into cash that very night. Somebody had advance notice of that consignment. How if Pippa gave them the tip-off?"

"Oh, *no*!" he said, with the last anguish on her account, and drew back his hands from the banknotes on the table. "You think this could be that money? After all this time?"

"No," said Bunty positively, "not that money. The last place they'd be likely to unload the goods and pick up the cash would be Comerbourne, where the stuff was consigned. No, not that. But supposing she'd been the contact for that. And supposing the same gang needed a safe deposit in Comerbourne on a later job, and thought they had a reliable little girl there—respectable, above suspicion, and already implicated in one affair. Because there *was* another gang job in Comerbourne, just three weeks ago. Didn't you hear about it? The pay-roll of Armitage Pressings was snatched on its way from the bank. The gang vanished, and so did the money. There were road-blocks up almost at once, but the money vanished, all the same. I reckon it vanished inside Comerbourne. Don't you? They found the van in a scrap-yard afterwards, right there in the town. The money had to lie somewhere until the heat was off. Deposited with some confederate inside the town, somebody they could trust. Somebody they *thought* they could trust. Armitage's pay-roll per week is around fifteen thousand. How much do you make this lot?"

He had been counting the number of notes in one bundle, and the number of bundles, but he couldn't believe the answer. " I figure it as something over fourteen thousand, anyhow. There'd be change, too, of course, if it was wages money, but that wouldn't be so portable, maybe she ditched that. Even the notes . . . but banks don't keep the numbers of the used notes they hand out, do they?"

The timing was right and the amount was right, and where else would a shop assistant get fifteen thousand pounds in notes? Bunty watched him fingering through the neat, banded bundles, still dazed. She saw his hand halt upon one of them, and his face grew sharply intent as he turned its edges towards him.

Black, rigid card—or was it a blue so dark as to be nearly black?—jutted on either side of the banknotes by a fraction of an inch. Luke had felt the alien stiffness even before he had seen the slivers of darkness. He thrust his thumb under the brown paper band and ripped it open, tumbling out upon the table a small black book, its cover printed in gilt lettering and heraldry between two white windows.

"A passport!"

Fire-new, virgin, its stiff cover opened a little as soon as the constriction was removed.

"Pippa's. Of course!" said Luke in a low voice, and opened it where the blue-tinted pages yielded of their own tension. Something folded double inside began to unfold in sympathy. "Aaaah!" he said in a long sigh. "Now I see!"

It was a B.E.A. ticket. He unfolded it and studied the details with a closed and unrevealing face.

"Dated for to-day. A single from Heath Row to Le Bourget. The eight o'clock Trident flight. So that's why she needed the Kwells! She'd have had to be at West London Air Terminal by seven o'clock. I don't suppose I should even have been awake by the time she took off for Paris. There wouldn't have been any difficulty. We . . . hadn't planned on sharing. . . . The only trick would have been getting this out of the tool-box while I wasn't around to see, and that wouldn't have bothered her. She'd only have to say she'd left something in the car, some time when I was shaving, or something, and couldn't run her errand myself. She could do harder things than that by far. And I don't suppose I was much of a problem to manage."

"No," agreed Bunty, "I don't suppose you were. But things didn't work out so easily. They came back for their money, just when she had everything planned for her run-out. What else could it be? They followed her to your house. Maybe they had someone watching her moves all along, those people don't trust anyone far. They saw her leaving with a suitcase, and followed her, and it would be simple enough getting into your place, even if the door was locked, but I don't suppose it was. . . ."

"It almost never was," he owned, fingering the air-line ticket sombrely on the table. "Sometimes not even when we went to bed. We hadn't anything worth stealing, we didn't think in terms of locking things up."

"So they just walked in. Just like Pippa. And they heard part—I'd say not very much—of what passed between you, and saw the struggle for the gun. How very easy, to knock you on the head, and then they could get rid of a liability and leave you to take the blame. When even you were convinced of your own guilt, why should the police look any farther? But you see where they went wrong. They were sure the money would be in Pippa's case. But it wasn't! And now it was too late to try and make her tell what she'd done with it. *They'd killed her!* She wasn't going to answer any questions any more. Probably they searched your cottage, but they can't have known about the car, waiting in the garage a whole street away, with this money packed inside it. They couldn't begin to guess where the loot really was. No! But they took her keys with them, and went back to make a thorough search of her flat. My guess is they'd take it for granted she'd moved the actual money, but they'd be looking for a left-luggage ticket, or a safe-deposit key, something that would show them where she'd hidden it."

He looked up at her, and his face warmed into a faint smile. "That's quite a lot of supposing."

"I know it is, but it adds up. And in that case we can be certain of one thing, the anonymous caller who alerted the police to come and fetch you *didn't* identify the corpse. They'd want the police busy round your place with everything they had. They wouldn't want any premature clue to send the investigation over to Pippa's flat, because they had a longish job of searching to do there themselves. And did you notice, none of these things in her bag has her name on it—not even in the purse, now I come to think of it."

"And now *I* come to think of it," he said, suddenly rearing his head like a hound pricking his ears at the distant sounds of the hunt, "they'd be expecting sensational news by this morning, a broadcast item about the murder at the least, police activity all round our quarter. And there wouldn't be any! They'd know it had gone wrong. They'd know I'd somehow managed to dispose of the body and get clean away."

Bunty made a soft, smothered sound of dismay. She got up quickly, beginning to thrust the bundles of notes together and fold the paper round them. "Yes . . . Luke, I hadn't thought . . . I didn't realise. . . ."

"And as they wouldn't find anything at Pippa's place," he said, "not even a left-luggage ticket, the next thought that would occur to them would be that I must have got away not only with Pippa and all the evidence, but also *with their fifteen thousand pounds.*"

CHAPTER IX

THEY STARED at each other across the table, across those absurd trivialities for which murder had been done, and the small, vicious personal treasons that make love unlovely; and each of them was furiously reckoning the risk to the other, and beginning to erect barricades.

"They'd be on the alert to-day," said Bunty, "for *any* police news from yesterday. There'll be nothing about murder, but they won't miss the significance of a car that went through a red light, and then nearly ran down a constable, because it was in such a guilty hurry to get away from Comerbourne."

"No," he agreed grimly, "they surely won't. The police up here were alerted, so there'll be something to give them the tip down there, even if it isn't exactly public yet. They'll know which way the police hunt has come. Within limits, they'll know where to look for me. . . ."

"For us," she said instantly.

"For *me*! Oh, Bunty . . . Oh, God, I ought to have sent you home!"

"You did try. Don't think of it, it isn't your fault that I wouldn't go. I wouldn't go even now," she said stubbornly.

" Then let's take all this stuff and get out of here, while the going's good. I want to get you to the police. I've never wanted the police so much," he said, and laughed rather breathlessly, tying the pink tape hurriedly round the parcel of notes. " Put your coat on," he said. " Never mind anything else, we'll bring them back here. *I'll* bring them back here. You'll stay where you're safe."

Yes, she thought, just get yourself and me into police hands, and I might even sit back and leave the rest to them, and to you.

" But we still have to avoid notice. The car . . ."

" It doesn't matter now," he said with decision. " If the police are on the look-out for me, so much the better, I'll gladly pull in and hand over to them. The others won't know details like our registration . . . or will they?" he wondered blankly, pulled up short at the thought of their complete isolation all day from the bulletins of the B.B.C. " Oh, lord, why doesn't Reggie put a proper radio in here? They bring the transistor, of course, damn the thing! We haven't a clue what they've been putting out all day, but I'll bet the gang have had a constant radio watch operating. You can pick up the police broadcasts, too, if you hunt round the wave bands. Many a time I've listened in to their two-way conversations about stolen cars. Ours is just the sort of item they'd be batting back and forth all day long."

" Those people may not be all that efficient," said Bunty scornfully, shrugging into her coat. She stooped to unplug the electric fire. " Don't forget the main switch, you know where it is, I don't. Look what a bad blunder they made, killing her. . . ."

He said: " Yes . . ." in so low and bitter a voice that she was suddenly visited by a private revelation of the love he had felt for that wretched girl upstairs, and the hooks it still had in his deepest sensitivities.

" Here, you have this!" He thrust the parcel of money upon her. " I'd rather . . . You found it. And you wouldn't believe," he said, " what a bad moment it gives you to have several thousand pounds of someone else's money in your hands, when you're broke every month-end without fail."

" It sticks to my fingers, too," she said, shaken by the knowledge that she was uttering no more than the truth. " Poor Pippa!" she added, and the connection was clear enough. " But we're luckier. It's better than fifteen thousand pounds to us, it's evidence for you."

The room looked as they had found it. When he threw the main switch there would be nothing but the tins and the broken china in the bin to show they had ever been here. Luke looked round him alertly, approved what he saw, and thrust the gun carefully into his right coat pocket, barrel foremost, a dormant devil. There remained, of course, out of sight but not out of mind, that pale blonde girl upstairs, impenetrably asleep in the pale blond room.

Outside the windows the world already looked dark; in reality it was no more than dusk. When they put out the lights within, the light without would revive and blossom almost into day.

Luke leaned into the broom cupboard, "Ready? I should get out to the front door, it'll seem dark at first. I'll bring a torch, there's one they keep in the store here."

She didn't move. She knew the geography of this house now rather better than that of her own. And she was going nowhere without him. Her honour was involved. What you pick up of your own will you can't in decency lay down. You must carry it as long as there's need, until it can stand alone, and walk alone, and not be challenged by anyone.

The light went out, and the window bloomed gradually into greenish, bluish pallor, lambent and enchanted, casting a faint gleam upon shapes inside the room. She waited with the flat packet under her arm, clutched tightly against her heart; and in a moment light, assured steps brought him to her side. A hand felt delicately in the gloom after her free hand, and found and clasped it.

And in that moment they heard it, the engine of the car that was winding its way cautiously along the sunken lane towards the house. A slow, sly, casing note, moving in methodically and without haste by the only approach, sure of closing the box on whatever was within. They heard it stop, somewhere round the curve of the grassland, beyond the trees. They stretched taller in the brief silence, waiting for it to start up again; and faithfully it throbbed into life and came on, with the deliberation of fate itself. Nearer now, but still with swelling ground between. But for the twilight silence it might have passed for traffic somewhere on the road, innocent and absorbed, not touching them.

Bunty thought hopefully, the police coming back. And as though she had spoken aloud, he said in a whisper: " No!" And after a moment of listening with held breath: " Not the same car."

He drew her out into the hall, and loosed her hand gently, and she heard him climbing the stairs in long, ranging, silent steps, three at a time. She groped her way after him, and found him in the large front bedroom, crouched at the window. Her eyes were already adjusting to the half-light, she could see clearly.

She saw the car creep very gently round the curve of the drive, shy in the shelter of the trees. She saw it halt to breathe, to observe the house in darkness, and then to accelerate and slide onward, reassured, into the gateway. Reassured? Or galvanised into more open action by fear that the place was indeed empty, that the birds were flown? It came on without concealment now, but quietly, hissed on to the edge of the gravel, rolled round before the door.

The doors of the car opened before it was still. Silently and purposefully two men slid out of it, one on either side, and then the motor cut out as suavely as a held sigh, and the driver slithered just as noiselessly from behind the wheel. Three figures, mute, shapeless and anonymous, deployed across the width of the gravel court, and looked up contemplatively under shading hat-brims at the blind front-

age of the house. And two of the figures, quite suddenly
and smoothly and naturally, as though these were the inevitable fruit you would expect to see ripening there, had
guns in their hands.

::   ::

Luke drew back from the window, caught Bunty in his
arm, and swept her away through the doorway to the landing, closing the door of the bedroom silently behind them.
Silence was everything now. Neither of them risked a
word, even in a whisper. Thank God they'd switched off
all lights before the car came within sight of the house. But
they were both remembering what the police sergeant had
said in the morning. He and his companion had seen a
light in one of the windows here "from up the coast road
a piece." So might these men have seen one, a quarter of
an hour ago. Bunty and Luke hadn't thought to be cautious about showing lights. Mrs. Chartley had reported her
presence to the police, so why disguise it? And now it was
too late to worry. Simply get out of here by the only remaining way, and pray that the searchers were merely following up one possibility, and would come to the conclusion
that the house was empty, and go away to hunt somewhere
else.

But the guns, flowering miraculously in hands that had
seemed to conjure them out of empty air, hadn't looked at
all tentative, or in the very slightest doubt of their premises.

Neither of them stumbled on the stairs, even in that
quietly frantic rush they made; neither of them fouled
any of the gay, impermanent fixings of the hall. They
could hear the faint, deliberate crunch of gravel under
cautious feet as the invaders cased the windows; but the
darkness inside was sufficient to swallow all movement, and
the glass in the panel of the front door was pebbled and
opaque without light to bring it to life. Luke felt his way
through the living-room door, and closed it gingerly after
them just as a hand eased up the latch of the front door,
with the faintest of metallic sounds, and tested it and found

it locked. After that they had more freedom to move, more insulation between themselves and their enemies, and they could concentrate on saving time, which was the most vital factor of all. They had to be well down the slate staircase to the inlet before the hunters found their way round the corner of the house to the rear terrace and the faint, lambent plane of the seascape beyond.

The boat was the only card they had left. Why, oh, why had she listened to her tidy, housekeeper's mind, and sent him to lock it away in the boat-house again? If it had still been riding at the jetty it would have saved them minutes now.

Out through the kitchen, out past the store, and Luke spared a moment to turn the key of the back door behind them. It slowed their retreat, but it completed the picture of an empty cottage, if only they could be far enough down the path to be out of earshot. There was no moon yet, but a faint starlight that brushed the flags of the tiny terrace, and gleamed on the level places in the pathway down the cliff. Thank God for the twists and turns in that erratic descent, that would take them out of sight within seconds. Sound would be a more dangerous betrayer.

Luke plunged to the edge of the terrace and led the way down in the dusk. He was on a path he knew, and could make good speed on the descent, but out of that complex of rocks the smallest rattle of a stone displaced would start a volley of rising echoes; and those characters out on the gravel weren't going to waste much time getting into the house. A shot will open a lock, if there's no other means at hand.

Luke put all thoughts out of his head for the moment, and concentrated on keeping his footing at a crazy speed, and bracing his left arm steadily to give Bunty a safety barrier from falling as she leaped and slid and bounded after him, and a grab handle whenever her foot stepped askew on the slates. The way was narrow as well as steep, his body would prevent her from crashing down towards the sea, even if she lost her footing. Whenever they reached one of the more level stretches he took her hand, but on the patches of broken shingle, laid with loose slate slabs for steps, she pressed close at his back and held by his shoulder. And at every step he quivered to the touch of her fingers with delight and agony, and wished her away, miles away in safety out of this mess in which he had involved her. But even then wishing her away was almost more than he could manage.

They were half-way down when he heard the back door of the cottage crash open above them, and at the same time the sound of running feet on the paved path that led round the house to the seaward side. One man had come round; two, probably, had gone through. Round the other end of the house it was impossible to go, it was built out to the edge of the drop. You could climb below safely enough if you had a fairish head for it, but not in the dark. Luke gripped the key of the boat-house in his pocket, his knuckles pressed for comfort against the gun. A finger of light from a torch fumbled down into the crevices of the rocks. They were sheltered from it by the tortuous turns, and close to the jetty now, but the pursuers could not fail to see the path, and the roof of the boat-house a sheen of grey in the sudden beam. With a light they could cover that descent only too quickly.

He was so intent on the movements of the men above that the movement below took him by surprise, bringing him up shocked and short like a blow to the heart.

A fourth man rose out of the shadows and bulked in their path darkly, blocking the way. The large, square-shouldered shape, neckless and muscular, closed the passage between the rocks solidly. A flat grey voice like the flat grey slates said: "Hold it right there, mate! Stay put, and get your hands up!"

Luke, arrested in mid-flight on steps steeper than average, pulled up with a suddenness that jarred him from heels to head, and cost Bunty her balance. Her foot slipped on a shifting stone, an unstable slate tilted forward as she stepped on it, and she was down on hands and knees, clinging to the rock, the displaced slab hard and heavy against her side. Some of the stones that supported its forward edge had rolled out of position and made it treacherous. She shoved her shoulder under it and heaved it back to its proper level to free herself of its weight, and the moment of confusion and alarm dissolved in understanding at that instant, and she knew they were not going to get away. They'd underestimated their opponents. The lay-out had been surveyed from the seaward side before ever the car drove up to the house. And this way, too, was closed to them.

She scrambled to her feet again, covered by Luke's body. She heard the hard voice below say impatiently: "You heard me, chum. Let's see your hands."

Luke fired from the pocket of his coat on the last word. He hadn't known he was going to do it, he hadn't even realised that his thumb had already shoved off the safety catch. Still less consciously had he calculated the angle of the drop before him, and tilted the thing well down in his pocket, to startle and cripple, perhaps, but not to kill. At this distance even he couldn't miss, the whole crevice between the rocks seemed to be full of the bulky body, with the lambent native silver of the sea outlining it clearly. He and Bunty had the dark and solid rock behind them; but even so, he reached for her with his left hand as he fired with the right, and drew her close to his back, covered from sight by his body.

The report was sharp and loud between the rocks, and followed closely by a gasping grunt and a curious, waspish whine. The dark shape before him buckled suddenly sideways, clutching at its knee, and went down in a toppling fall on to the stones, sliding downhill a yard with scrambling feet before it found a stable resting-place. What astonished Luke most was that the other gun didn't go off, but he had no time to speculate on the reason. Without a word he launched himself forward down the path, swung

Bunty before him past the grovelling, groaning, cursing
man on the ground, and charged after her.

The threshing shape heaved suddenly, as if the rock had
risen under him; an arm came up and reached for him. He
hurdled the body blindly, felt the fingers claw at his ankle
and miss their hold. Then he came down by ill luck on
shifting stones that rolled away from under his foot and
flung him on his back, knocking the breath out of him, and
half the sense with it. The hand that had missed his ankle
scrabbled after him hungrily, and found a grip on his hair.
A solid weight rolled over on top of him, holding him
down; the hand shifted to his mouth. Not to his throat, his
mouth! That was it, that was why no shot, either, he
realised, struggling to free his arms from the weight that
pinned them. They wanted no sound carrying for miles
up-coast and down over the sounding-board of this placid
sea. This back-gate guard had been told to threaten, not to
fire. In that case Luke had good reason to be glad of his
own single shot; someone, somewhere, might have heard.
Bunty, he thought desperately, wrenching one arm clear
and jabbing upwards viciously under a thick jaw, scream,
now, while you've got the chance, and keep on screaming.
They might cut and run yet. But what was the use, she
wasn't a screamer. Not a sound from her!

An arm swung at his head, and he rolled aside from
the blow and felt something hard graze his temple and
clang like metal on the rock. Whalebone fingers ground
deep into his cheeks, clamping his lips against his teeth. He
fought for breath, and heard his opponent pumping in sobbing gasps of air and spending them in incoherent, mono-
tonous curses, hissing with pain between the words that
were hardly words. When the weight on top of him
shifted for another attempt at clubbing him with the
gun, he heaved up one knee and tried to throw his incubus
from him, but it was too heavy to be lifted or unbalanced
so easily. And from somewhere above, a crazy accom-

paniment to this disordered scene, came the busy, absorbed sound of feet descending endlessly towards them, like the Goons padding along some impossibly long radio corridor to open the door to one more visitor to Bedlam.

It was Bunty, however, who reached them first, Bunty with a sizable stone in her two hands, and some furious atavism stirring in her that made fear of secondary importance. It was not a particularly well-chosen stone, but she had had to grope for it in the dark. Nor was she very deft at using it; perhaps she was right, and they both of them had some built-in prohibition against killing that handicapped them badly in a situation like this. But she did her best. The stone thudded against the back of a classically Alpine skull, low towards where the neck should have been if there had been any neck, and rolled down hunched shoulders to bounce away down the slope. The throttling hand slackened, the weight slumped with a grunt over Luke's threshing body. Bunty, taking what she could find, reached over the wide shoulders to seize the lapels of the man's raincoat, and drag it back with all her strength to pinion his upper arms. Luke heaved himself clear with a convulsion that sent them all three slipping and staggering downhill; and Bunty caught at his hand and helped to pull him to his feet.

They were at the edge of the jetty, hand in hand, the injured man dragging himself along after them half-stunned and moaning, when the three men from above overtook and fell upon them. Luke, swinging to fight them off a shade too late, went down heavily beneath two of them, and stayed down. Bunty, turning at the edge of the water, watched the small, murderous black eye of a revolver advance at leisure until it touched her breast.

"All right, sweetheart," said the small, murderous, black-a-vised man behind the gun, in just the mild, metallic, indifferent voice the gun might have used, "upstairs again, and see and be a lady on the way. Your boy-friend here

can't afford no slips on your part. He's got enough troubles
as it is. Walk!"

: :   : :

Bunty walked, at an even and sedate pace, leading that
procession up the cliff-path and back to the house, with
the gun not a yard from her back, and a torch pricking
her consciousness occasionally to remind her that every step
was watched. She walked with the same erect stride she
always had, stretching her long legs to the steeper steps
without slackening speed. There was nothing she could
do, except make it clear that she had no tricks to play.
Luke was only a few yards behind her, and the enemy,
though reduced to three against two, had now four guns at
their disposal, and none ranged against them. There was
no sense in provoking death.

Far behind them among the rocks, the wounded man
hoisted himself painfully from stair to stair, dragging one
leg and leaving a long smear of blood behind him. When
the prisoners were safely in the house and under guard, perhaps one of his fellows would help him to finish the journey. Now it seemed that he was of no importance. His
thin, quiet cursing followed them up to the terrace, and
behind it like a backcloth rolled the soft, absorbed night-
singing of a calm sea.

How queer, thought Bunty involuntarily, I still don't
know where we are. Somewhere on the east coast of Scotland. North of Muirdrum, I remember the policeman
there thought he'd recognised Luke's car passing through.
Luke mentioned going into Forfar. Her mind sketched in,
with lightheaded clarity, a map of the Angus coastline.
Somewhere between Arbroath and Montrose? Up the
coast there must be Lunan Bay, and farther north are the
Bullars of Buchan, where Doctor Johnson insisted on
sailing into the rock cauldron in a small boat. You can
only do it when it's calm. *Calm!* Like to-night. You
could do it to-night.

Luke came up the path after her between two guns. The

key of the boat-house had been taken from him along with
the gun from the same pocket. All their evidence lost. He
was bruised, sore and sick with chagrin; but most of all
he raged that he had not sent Bunty home or taken her
to the safety of the nearest police station in the morning,
while there'd been time, time they'd frittered away in supposing that they had only the police to contend with. Now
they knew better, and now was too late.

But at every step he felt that there was something wrong,
that something about Bunty was not as he had expected it
to be, and his battered and confused mind could not run
the discrepancy to earth. Not until they were hustled and
prodded through the back door into the kitchen, and there
penned in a corner until someone found the fuse-box. The
wounded man, out in the darkness, laboriously groaned
and fumbled his way up towards the terrace, and no one
seemed to care. If you're incapacitated, you're finished
with. Throw the broken one away and get a new one. The
modern trend even with human beings, it seemed. Luke
shivered, but even in the middle of this horror there was
a grain of comfort that glowed securely, so clear was the
division between himself and these people with whom, for
a while, he had been confusing himself.

It was worth finding out, even if it was the last thing he
did.

"Draw the curtains," ordered the irresponsibly cheerful
voice from inside the broom-cupboard. "Don't want to
embarrass the visitors, do we? Neighbours are nosy enough
without encouraging 'em." A curious, high-pitched giggle
echoed brassily out of the enclosed space.

"They're drawn," said the small, dark, deadly one.
"Get on with it."

"All right, the current's on."

The third man flipped down the light-switch, the round
fluorescent fixture blinked its daylight eye once, and then
glowed steadily. And there they were, all five of them,
two prisoners and three captors. No, six altogether, the

lame man was just fumbling his way through the doorway, holding by the latch with all his weight. They hauled
him inside not out of any concern for him, but so that they
could close the door and keep the light within.

It was then that Luke realised at last what had been
wrong with Bunty. How could she have used both hands
to heave up that rock and crack this wretch on the head
with it? She'd been carrying something when they set out.
She wasn't carrying anything now, except the handbag
that swung from her wrist. She had both hands in the
pockets of her light grey coat, and was looking round at
them all measuringly and warily, her face stonily calm.
She met even his eyes, and her expression didn't change,
was significantly careful not to change.

Somewhere, at some moment which he could not locate
in his frantic recapitulation, Bunty had disposed of the
better part of fifteen thousand pounds. The package of
banknotes and Pippa Gallier's passport and air ticket had
vanished without trace.

CHAPTER X

"Nothing else on either of 'em," reported the giggler,
shoving Luke back into the corner of the wicker settee with
a careless vigour that made the white frame creak indignantly. "Never thought there would be. I told you these
babes are sharper than he reckoned."

So there was another he, not so far present. They had
been gradually coming to some such conclusion. Why
should all hands have kept off them so indifferently,
otherwise? The one who called the tune wasn't here yet.
These four were merely waiting, and filling in time with
the necessary preliminaries while they waited.

Bunty and Luke sat side by side in the two-seater settee,
pushed well back into the window embrasure, as far as possible from the door of the living-room. It was easy for one

man to control them there. The third man, the youngest, the dimmest, but perhaps the most vicious, too, sat on a chair placed carefully before them, far enough away to be out of their reach, close enough to have them both infallibly covered. He held his gun as though he loved it, as a call-girl might hold diamonds, and his eyes above it were like chips of bluish stone, flat and impervious, a little mad, the cunningly inlaid eyes of a stone scribe from later Egypt, built up with slivers of lapis lazuli and onyx and mother-of-pearl to give a lifelike semblance of humanity. He was dressed in what his kind and generation would certainly classify as sharpish gear, and he couldn't have been more than twenty-one. Bunty, watching him, sat very still indeed. The little dark man would kill for what seemed to him sufficient reason, and without any qualms except for his own safety afterwards. The other two would probably kill if they were ordered to. But this young one was the kind that might go off without warning, like a faulty grenade, and kill to ease his tension, or relieve his boredom, or simply because it occurred to him momentarily as something it would be fun to do, and no consideration of his own safety would keep him back, because thought had nothing to do with his processes.

The giggler could have passed for normal any time he liked. He was big and rosy, and looked like a country butcher, well-fleshed but not yet run to fat. There was nothing at all suspect about him, except the slightly hysterical pitch of his laughter.

And the other man, the one who had been posted well down the rock path to intercept them, sat hunched in one of the big chairs now, with his left trouser-leg rolled up above the knee, painfully sponging at his calf, where Luke's shot had torn its way straight through to ricochet from the rock behind. He had bled a lot, the water in the bowl at his feet was red. He pawed self-pityingly at the thick white flesh, and took no notice of what the others were doing. The giggler had fetched down gauze and wool and a bandage for him from the bathroom cupboard, and the victim was totally absorbed in nursing his wound. And indeed, thought Bunty, eyeing the damage, he must have been in a good deal of pain. When he had finished his bandaging, and got up gingerly to try his weight on the injured leg, all he could manage was a slow hobble, clinging to the furniture for support.

He was the biggest of them, and the oldest, a massive, muscular person with a white, sad, fleshy face. His hair was receding, and his expression was anxious and defensive. The small dark one had called him Quilley. There was something odd in the attitude of the younger ones to him, the way they left him out of their calculations, or included him only as an afterthought. Or perhaps it was not so odd, in such a world as theirs, that a man's stock should crash when he's disabled, or has got the worst of an encounter. He was a doubtful asset now, and a potential liability. Some wild animals, the kind that hunt in packs, kill off their injured or infirm members, as some sort of measure of social hygiene.

" It's here, though," said the small dark man with certainty. " It's here somewhere. Either we find it, or he tells us where. The place ain't that big. You sure about the car, then, Skinner?"

" I'm sure," said the giggler cheerfully, spinning the garage key round his finger with absent-minded dexterity. " Clean as a whistle."

" You didn't miss out on anywhere? Under the back seat? Down the upholstery?"

" I didn't miss out on anything. There's nothing there."

" What you wasting time for?" the boy with the levelled gun demanded querulously, without removing his unwinking stone gaze from his charges. " I could get it out of him easy. Or *her*!" The flick of excitement on the last word indicated that he would rather prefer that alternative. Bunty supposed that in its obscene fashion it was a compliment, but if so, it was one she could well have done without. She could feel Luke's muscles stiffening beside her, his whole body rigid with anxiety. She cast one glance at him, and found his fixed profile almost too still. The cheek nearer to her was bruised and soiled. His mouth was drawn and stiff with fear for her.

"Yeah, I know!" said the dark man sardonically. "And all at once we got no clues and no witness. If anybody shuts *this* one's mouth for good, it ain't going to be while *I*'m in charge. Think the boss'd wear that from anybody but himself? Sooner you than me, mate! But till he gets here, you take orders from me, and my orders are, *lay off*. OK?"

"Well, OK, Blackie, it's all one to me. I'm only saying . . ."

"You always are. Quit saying, and just keep your eye on 'em, that's all, while we take this room apart." He cast a long look round the airy living-room, and ended eye-to-eye with Luke. He wasn't expecting anything to come easily, but he went through the motions of asking. "You could make it easy on yourself and us, kid. In the end you may have to, you know that? What *did* you do with the money?"

"What money?" said Luke.

Skinner, dismantling the drawers of the writing-desk one by one, giggled on his unnerving high note. "Get that! He knows nothing about any money. *What money!*"

"All right," said Blackie, sighing. "You want it the hard way, you can have it. We've got time. But don't say I didn't ask you nicely. If you think better of it, just say, any time. We're going to find it in the end."

And they set to work to find it, emptying books from the shelves, letters from the bureau, rolling back the rugs for loose blocks in the parquet, but discovering none. They took the living-room to pieces and put it together again, neatly and rapidly but without haste, with the thoroughness of long practice. But they found nothing of interest. And Bunty and Luke, so close to each other that their arms

brushed at every slight movement, sat and watched the
search with narrow attention, and kept silent. They had
nothing to say in these circumstances, even to each other.
They hardly ventured to look at each other, for fear even
that exchange should give something away. Yet something had passed between them, tacitly and finally. Neither
of them would dream of giving in, unless or until the case
was beyond hope. Perhaps not even then; they were both
stubborn people. He didn't know what Bunty had done
with the parcel of notes, but if she'd had the presence of
mind to hide it even out there in the dark, pursued and
ambushed as they'd been, then she certainly wasn't going
to give away its whereabouts now without the toughest of
struggles. And Luke couldn't because he didn't know.

"Clean as wax-polish in here," concluded Blackie, looking round the room. "Let's have a go at the kitchen."

The kitchen, compact though it was, was full of fitments
that would keep them busy for quite a while. Blackie sized
up the job in one frowning stare, and jerked his head at
the youth guarding the prisoners.

"Hey, you, Con . . . hand over to Quilley and come
and give us a hand here."

"What, and leave nobody but him between this lot and
the front door?" Con said disrespectfully. "With the lock
broke? Or did you forget?"

With impassive faces and strained senses Bunty and Luke
filed away for reference one more scrap of information that
might, just might, with a lot of luck, be relevant and useful. They'd had to break the lock to get in. The bolts
hadn't been shot, so there might still be those to contend
with, supposing a chance ever offered; but on the whole
it was unlikely that they would have bothered to shoot them
home now. They were expecting the boss; and the boss
sounded the sort of man who would expect all doors to
open before him without delay.

"Watch it!" said Blackie, without personal animosity.
"You're nearly too fly to live with, these days, you are.

So if he can't sprint, he'll still have a gun, won't he?"

"Yes, and instructions not to do any real damage with it!"

Con talked too much for his own good. That little weakness might have been there to be discovered in any case, but there'd been no need to spell it out and underline it. For the sake of the information they—or one of them—held, Bunty and Luke must at all costs be preserved alive until they had confided it. Once the secret had been prised out of them, of course, they were expendable enough.

"What if they jump him? So he plugs one of 'em in the leg, and the other's out of the room and out the front door, and us all back there in the kitchen. And that'll sound good when you make your report, Blackie, me old Crowe."

"All right, then, we'll make dead sure. Bring 'em in here with you, and lock 'em in the store. There's no window in there, and only one door, and that's into the kitchen. That'll make four of us between them and any way out. Satisfied?"

"Whatever you say." Con rose, unfolding his long legs and arms with the stiffly articulated movements of a grasshopper. He made a brisk upward gesture with the gun. "Come on, then, let's have the pair of you. You heard the gentleman. You want showing the way to the store? Hey, Blackie, there's nothing useful in there, is there? Garden shears or sécateurs, or like that?"

"Nah, nothing, we done in there. Bring 'em along!"

"After *you*, lady!" said Con with a whinnying laugh, and ground the barrel of his revolver hard into Luke's ribs out of sheer exuberance. From his chair Quilley watched them go with harassed, apathetic eyes, as if he had resigned perforce from the whole business, and was waiting with apprehension for someone to decide what was to be done with him now.

All Mrs. Alport's primrose-coloured kitchen fitments stood open, and the giggler was grubbing among the taps under the sink. The store measured only three feet by two, and some of that was taken up by shallow shelves at the back, where Reggie Alport kept his electrical spares, bulbs, fuse-wire, plugs and adaptor. Luke had to stoop to enter it; even Bunty's hair brushed the roof.

Con watched them fold themselves uncomfortably and closely together in this upright coffin, and shrilled with horse-laughter as he closed and locked the door on them.

"Nice and cosy for two . . . I call that just the job. Hey, Blackie, I hope you know what you're doing. I can't see 'em wanting to come out o' there." He thumped the locked door just once with the flat of his hand. " Have fun!" he called, and went off to sack Louise Alport's cupboards.

: :   : :

In the darkness, smelling of timber and fine dust, Luke shifted gently to make more room for her, and drew her closely into his arms; there was no other way of finding adequate space. Her head fitted into the hollow of his shoulder and neck; she felt his cheek pressed against her hair, and his lips close to her ear.

"Bunty. . . ." The finest ardent thread of a whisper. " Did you understand? They can't lock the front door, they had to break the lock. Bunty, I'm going to try to start something . . . the first chance I get, when they fetch us out of here. . . ."

" No," she breathed into his ear as softly and us urgently, " you mustn't. They'll shoot you . . ."

" Not until they've found out what they want. They don't want to go to extremes until *he* gets here. You heard them. They as good as said *he*'s already rubbed out one person too soon, before he got his questions answered. Bunty, I'm going to try it. What else is there for us? I'll try to give you the item, but when I cut loose, *you run*. . . ."

" No!" she said, an almost soundless protest.

" *Yes*. I'll cover you . . . somehow I will. You go straight for the front door and out. And, Bunty . . . don't stay on the road, *get into the trees*. . . . This lot are car men, cross-country you can leave them standing. . . ."

" I'm not going," she said.

"*Yes* . . . you've *got* to go. You can go to the police, then, you can tell them. I'll stick it out here till they come."

" In what sort of shape?" she whispered bitterly.

" Alive . . . and not a murderer. Better shape than I was in this time last night."

" But Luke, listen . . . the police have had time by now to check up on that name and address I gave them. Suppose they do? Suppose they find out your friends have never heard of me, and the address I gave doesn't exist? They'll be back to find out what I'm up to, what's going on here. This is the one place they'll make for—*they'll* come to *us*. They could be back any moment," she said, and her breath was warm on his cheek, turning his heart faint and crazed with love.

" Yes, they could," he said, and his whispering voice trembled with the effort it put into being convincing; but she knew he didn't believe in it.

Neither did she, altogether, but it was at least a possibility. Especially if, by any remote chance, someone had brought in that purse with Bunty Felse's name on it, and tried to return it, and so set the Midshire police hunting for a missing woman, whose description would fit the totally unexpected woman in the Alports' cottage here in Angus. Such a long and complicated " if "; but no one is more likely to fit diverse pieces of a puzzle patiently together than the police, whose job it is. And no one has better communications.

" But I want you out," he said, " before it comes to shooting. Even if they do come, it might be touch and go. I'd rather get you away. If I can make that chance, promise to try . . . promise me, Bunty. . . ."

She lifted a hand and touched his cheek gently, let her palm lie there for a long moment holding him, partly in apology, partly as a distraction, because she had no intention of making any promises. When the time came she would play it as seemed best, weighing the chances for

him as well as she could in the split second she would have
for consideration. But she could not conceive of any com-
bination of circumstances that was likely to induce her to
leave him now.

He wanted to turn his head the few necessary inches, and
press his lips into her palm, but he didn't do it, because he
had no rights in her at all but those she had given him
freely, and they were not that kind of rights. Until they
were out of here—if they ever got out of here alive—there
was nothing he could say to her, though his heart might
be bursting. Afterwards, if they could clear up this affair
with all its debts and start afresh, things might go very
differently. But the darkness in which they stood seemed
to him a symbolic as well as an actual darkness, and he
couldn't see anything ahead. And there might not be any
more time for talking, to-night or ever.

"Bunty, I'm sorry!" he breathed, and that seemed to be
it. He had never been so short of words, and in any case,
what good were they?

"For what? For getting into a mess through no real
fault of your own?"

"For everything I've done to you. For involving you. I
wish I could undo it," he said. "Forgive me!"

"There's nothing to forgive. You couldn't have involved
me if I hadn't involved myself. No debts either way.
Simply, it happened."

"No . . . I began as your . . . murderer . . ." The
word was almost inaudible, lost in the tangle of her hair.
"Don't let me end like that now. I'll make the chance
and you must go. That's why you *must* . . . I can bear it
if *you* get back safely . . . I'll be satisfied then."

And he meant it. If she had come out like a pilgrim,
looking for something uniquely her own, some justification
of her whole life to show to the gate-keepers and the gods
when her time came, she had it. For every journey, even
the last one, you need a ticket.

::   ::

The dulled accompaniment of voices and movements from the kitchen had halted, recommenced, changed, and the two of them in their narrow prison had never noticed. Nor could they hear the approach of the car through so many layers of insulation. The first they knew of the boss's arrival was when the door of the store-cupboard was suddenly flung open, and Skinner beckoned them out into the light. They came, dazzled for a while after such a darkness, eyes wide and dazed from staring into a different kind of light. Luke kept his arm about Bunty as they were herded through the kitchen and into the living-room.

And the living-room was full of a large, restless, top-heavy man in a light overcoat and a deeper grey suit, standing astride the orange-coloured rug. It was a still night, but he seemed somewhere to have found a reserve of tempestuous wind, and brought it into the house in the folds of his well-tailored but untamed clothes, so that the room seemed suddenly gusty and tremulous, convulsed with the excess of his energy. He was nearly half a head taller than Luke, and twice as wide, massive shoulders and barrel chest tapering away to long, narrow flanks. For all that bulk, he moved with a violent elegance that was half exuberant health and half almost psychotic self-confidence and self-love. He straddled the floor and looked them all over with the eye of a proprietor, viewing a new acquisition which didn't look like much now, but of which he could make something in double-quick time, and something profitable, too.

His head was big, to match his shoulders, and startlingly rough-hewn after the disguise of his immaculate clothes ended at the collar; a head of crude, bold lines, and a face in which the bone strained glossy beneath the tanned skin, not because there was so little flesh there, but because there was so much bone. He had a forehead ornamented with knobbly projections like incipient horns, and above it bright auburn hair grew low to a widow's peak. An upright cleft marked his massy chin. The deepset eyes—boxers should

have eyes like that, invulnerable, lids and all, in cages of
concrete skull, cased with hide like polished horn—twinkled
with restless, reddish lights, good-humoured without being
in the least reassuring.

... *auburn hair growing low, cleft chin, eyes buried in
a lot of bone* ...

Luke's fingers closed meaningly on Bunty's arm. He
couldn't say anything to her, but there was no need, he had
described this man to her so well that even she knew him
on sight. This was the man on whose arm Pippa Callier
had leaned devotedly as they left her flat together on
Friday night, the man whose car had stood all night in the
mews round the corner, waiting to take a mythical mother
and her mythical cousin home again to Birmingham. How
strange that she should have thought she could get away
with such a pretence, even for a moment. And how innocent and unpractised it suddenly made her in Bunty's sight.
This was nobody's cousin, and one could almost believe,
nobody's son. He could have burst out of a rock somewhere of his own elemental force, self-generated and dangerous.

She pressed her elbow into Luke's side in acknowledgment. But there was no way of telling him that she suddenly found herself better informed even than he was, that
she, too, had seen this man before, just once and briefly,
too distantly to have known all those details of his appearance, but clearly enough to know his movements again
wherever she saw them, the long, arching stride of a man
with vigour to spare, the appraising tilt of the big head,
the swinging use of the high shoulders. On Friday evening,
when he had meant nothing to her, before he changed
into the dinner jacket that Luke had found so conspicuous
in Queen Street.

Luke knew the boss's face again, as he had said he would.
But Bunty knew more, his trade, his provenance, even his
name, that last magic that every elemental being should
guard as he guards his life, for in a sense it *is* his life.

This one hadn't guarded his. He had had it printed on windscreen stickers, blazoned on fluorescent posters, strung along thirty-seven be-flagged frontages in neon lights for all the world to see and memorise.

His name was Fleet.

CHAPTER XI

THE HUGE NEWCOMER revolved on the heel of a hand-made shoe, taking in all the inhabitants of this minor kingdom of his, and dealing in turn with them all.

"Hah!" he said, a bark of satisfaction and amusement, as he surveyed Luke from head to foot with one flash of his coarse-cut-marmalade eyes. "I see you got the right party, anyhow. That's something!"

The snapping gaze swept over Bunty with interest, sized her up with casual appreciation, and flicked another glance at Luke. "Well, get that! He finds new ones fast. Who'd have thought it!"

He tossed the key he was swinging across to Skinner. "Turn the Jag round, will you, and wheel it up to the gate ready for off. You never know, we might have to leave on the hop."

The skirt of his pearl-grey Terylene overcoat whirled, and another spin brought him to Quilley. "What's the matter with *you*?" There was no sympathy in the inquiry, rather a note of outrage, even of immediate reserve. His employees had no business to get hurt on duty.

"I stopped one, boss. He had a gun."

"Couldn't you bet on him having a gun?" Bunty had the impression for one instant that he had almost said "*The* gun", and thought better of it in time. "What's up, then? How bad is it?" The top span, and he confronted Blackie. "If he's a write-off for anything active, we can use him upstairs. Why haven't you got someone up there keeping a watch out? I tell you, half the constabulary could be walking in on us, and you sitting here playing hide and seek."

"Somebody'd have been up there any minute now," said Blackie, without noticeable chagrin; and indeed, the big man's voice, vibrant, full and pleasantly pitched, had no displeasure in it, he flashed and fulminated from excess of energy, and took delight in it as a kind of self-expression.

"Yeah, I know, because you cleaned up down here! All right, then, Quilley, get up there and keep a watch out front and back both. You can take it easy up there, just so you don't miss any movements around this place."

"He can start looking around inside, too," said Blackie. "Because it ain't in here, it ain't in the kitchen or back there. And these two are playing dumb and daft."

"It has to be somewhere here. Stands to sense. Go take that little front room apart, Skinner, and then go up and join Quilley. If he's there by then." He cast a thoughtful eye at Quilley's painful and laborious progress across the room and out to the stairs. "They get old and slow," said Fleet with tolerant regret, like a practical farmer contemplating putting down a worn-out horse. And he peeled off his smart driving gloves, dove grey and tan, and dropped them on the table, beside the scattered belongings they had taken from Luke's pockets.

"These what were on him?" He pawed them over thoughtfully. "Keys . . . several. His own bunch . . . house . . . car . . . suitcase? That'll be upstairs . . . or had he got it away somewhere?"

"It's upstairs. They never had time to take anything with 'em, they just ran when they heard us. There's a way down to the water, and a boat-house down there. Locked. I reckon this would be the key to that. He had it in his coat pocket, along with the gun. This one's the back door. We sprung that, it was an easy touch. The front we had to bust."

"And what's this other one?"

Echoing hollowly down the wall of the stairs dead on cue, Quilley's voice, dutifully anxious to please, reported: "Boss, there's one of these bedrooms locked up." He was hopeful of a discovery. A locked door was promising.

"That'll be it," said Fleet, pleased. "There's a key here could belong to it," he called. "Skinner, come and take it up to him, see what he's got there. And better have a quick look through the suitcase."

Skinner came at leisure, cheerful as ever; it began to seem a lunatic cheerfulness.

"And now," said Fleet, dusting his hands, "suppose you two sit down prettily over there, where we can keep an eye on you, and we'll have our little talk."

He caught a dining-chair by the back, and swung it into a reversed position in front of the wicker settee, to which Con had again herded his prisoners. The light skirts of the pearl-grey coat whisked out like wings. Fleet sat down astride the chair, and leaned his folded arms comfortably on the back.

"Straight to the point, that's me. *Where's the money?*"

"What money?" said Luke woodenly. "I know nothing about any money."

"Pippa Gallier didn't bring any money over to my place Saturday evening. I'm a reasonable man, I'll try to help you remember."

"Pippa Gallier didn't bring any money over to my place Saturday evening," said Luke. "You're barking up the wrong tree."

"Kiddo, she sure as fate didn't bring it Friday evening, but who's arguing about dates? She brought it. She was shinning out, and you were the ferryman. You may as well tell me now what you've done with it, because I'm going to find out in the end."

"She never brought any money to me, I'm telling you."

"You're telling me fairy-tales, kid, but go ahead. I've got time."

Uninvited, Bunty said in a hard, detached voice:

"That's what you think. But what you don't know is that the police have been here before you. This morning. I got rid of them then, but what I told them isn't going to last them long. My bet is they could be back any moment now. I expected them before this. You don't think this place *belongs* to him, do you?"

Fleet turned his head the little way that was necessary, and gave her his full attention for the first time. She sat with fixed, motionless face, smoothing a chipped nail on one hand, but at Fleet's persistent stare she raised to him the full hazel glance of her eyes, wide and unwavering.

"You know," said Fleet, "you're not at all hard to look at, now I come to notice, but girl, you're no hand at lying."

"That makes it even funnier," said Bunty, unmoved, "because I'm not lying. But you know it all. Don't say I didn't warn you."

It was essential that none of these men should suspect how easy it would be to wring concessions from her by tormenting Luke, or from Luke by tormenting her. She had even toyed momentarily with the idea of trying to act the part of a disillusioned pick-up with cheapened accent and roughened voice, but she knew she couldn't make a job of it. And it occurred to her now that that might not have confused Fleet in the slightest, while this more unexpected female companion put him slightly off his immaculate stride. And all the while she was straining her ears after what was happening upstairs. Maybe they were turning out Luke's suitcase first, as the best bet. But the discovery couldn't be long now. Her nerves tightened, waiting for it.

"And where," inquired Fleet curiously, "did he find you? It sure didn't take him long. I wouldn't have thought he was that quick off the mark."

"I picked her up in a pub," Luke said harshly. "I should have left her there."

The words were acknowledgment enough of the lead she had given him, and fitted the image of indifference now turning to resentment. It was lucky that they were also true, Bunty thought, for up to then she had no great opinion of Luke's potentialities as a liar.

And it was at that moment that the pair upstairs un-locked the door of the guest bedroom, and walked in upon the treasure secreted there.

The cry that came hollowly down the stairs was almost a scream, brief, horrified and unreasonably alarming. Fleet came to his feet in a cat's alert, hair-triggered leap, whirl-ing the chair away from him across the room. Blackie span round to face the doorway, gun in hand. Con kept his weapon levelled, but even his stony eyes wandered. It was the first moment of disarray, and it was useless. Three here between the prisoners and the door, two more scuttling in haste down the stairs to add to the odds. Luke's braced muscles ached with longing, but he knew it was no good. He would only succeed in killing them both.

" For Pete's sake . . . !" exploded Fleet exasperatedly. " What's with you two?"

Skinner appeared in the doorway, mouth and eyes wide open, with Quilley limping and shivering at his back.

" In that room, the locked one . . . You know what's in there, boss? *She* is . . . the Gallier girl! He brought her up here with him! She's there lying on the bed!"

:: ::

Fleet struck his large, well-kept hands together with a clap like a gun going off and uttered a brief crow of amusement, astonishment and triumph.

" And her things? Is her case here?"

" It's there." Blackie indicated the corner where it stood against the wall. " Her bag, too, it's there on the bookcase. We started with them, but there's nothing . . . Well, we *knew* . . ." He swallowed that admission in time. " But I never thought he'd bring *her* all the way up here. I thought he'd ditched her somewhere. . . ."

Fleet came strolling back across the room like a con-tented cat, long-stepping, disdainful, spread his feet wide before his prisoners, and leaned over them with a benign smile.

"So you don't know anything about my money, eh? And I take it you know nothing about the girl up there, either? She just flew here! As for the police, they kindly called in this morning, I suppose, and helped you carry her upstairs? Now we know where we stand."

He plucked back the chair, span it about in one hand, and resumed his place astride it in high good-humour; and the trouble was that Bunty could not for the life of her see how his mind was working. Something obscure and complicated was going on in that formidable skull, something of no advantage to anyone but himself, something that involved and made sense of the body upstairs, and still left him free. He'd admitted nothing, except that he was looking for the money; and such indiscretions as the others had let fall didn't amount to much, and in any case, she realised with a small leap of her heart, he didn't know about them, and was planning whatever he was planning without taking them into account. He was *pleased* about Pippa being here in the house, it had suggested something to him, something neat and workmanlike that afforded for him an effective exit. Bunty wished she knew what it was.

"So you brought her body up here, and all her things, and left the deck clean. Nobody could blame you for that, either, kid, nor for bringing the money along, too. Where was it? Not in her case, I know that . . . I was looking for it, while you were still out cold . . . *right after you shot her.* . . ."

His voice moved like a cat, too, suavely and softly and bonelessly along the insinuating sentences, and pounced suddenly, a fishing cat. But the flashing paw clawed up more than he had bargained for. Until that moment it had not dawned on either of his listeners that he might well be in doubt as to how much Luke knew about the events of Saturday night, and how guilty he believed himself to be. A little push in the right direction might get him the information he needed. But it was a chance two could take; and the right reaction might even provide them with a slender and precarious advantage.

Luke closed his eyes and sank his head in his hands. He made no attempt to deny anything. Bunty held her breath, feeling her way after him blindly.

" So I reckon the money was in the one place I couldn't get at. *In the car.* . . ."

" The car's clean," said Blackie. " Skinner took it apart."

" *Now* it's clean. But that's where the stuff was. Must have been. We looked everywhere else. So you found it, kiddo, and you were all set to make a clean get-away with it, is that it? After all, you had to run, they'd soon be after you for murder. Better run with a nice little nest-egg like that than without it. You know what, I've got a lot of sympathy for you! She was a crooked little bitch, if ever there was one. Crossed you up for me, and crossed me up for the money I trusted her with. She asked for what you gave her. If it hadn't been you it would have been someone else. The way I felt when I found she'd cut and run with my money, I tell you straight, it might have been *me* if you hadn't got in first."

" I was drunk," protested Luke from behind his sheltering hands, and the dark hair shook forward over his brow and helped to hide his face. His voice was high and unsteady, it would do well enough for an ordinary, harmless young man who had been running all day from the nightmare knowledge that he was a murderer. " I didn't even *know*," he said, writhing. " She waved the damn gun at me . . . she made me mad. . . ."

" I know! She asked for it. I'm not planning on turning you in for that."

Not this time, thought Bunty; because you've thought of something better. I wish I knew what it is! I wish I knew, I wish Luke knew, exactly how much of that quarrel you did overhear.

Luke looked up mistrustfully under his disordered hair. The big man loomed over him mountainous and daunting, his face in shadow.

" What were you planning on doing? . . . you and the lady? I hear there's a boat . . . was that it? You reckon you could make it across to the Continent from here?"

"Yes, I could make it . . . I *could* have made it," Luke corrected himself bitterly, " if you hadn't sent this lot after us."

" And Pippa? She was going half-way, I suppose?"

The dark head drooped again, the thin hands came up and scrubbed wearily at the thin cheeks. An almost inaudible voice said : " Yes. . . ."

" Look," said Fleet reasonably, " I'm not a cop. I've got nothing against you. Why should I have? She did the dirty on both of us, I've got a fellow feeling for you. There's no reason in the world why you and I shouldn't do a deal."

He was, in his way, a marvellous performer. To look at him sitting there, his rocky face placid and benevolent, was almost to believe in his genuineness. He could create a kind of hallucination even when you knew he was lying, by the sheer force of his energy. Yet at the same time he had produced on Bunty an effect for which not even she was prepared. Up to now she had merely reasoned that this man had killed Pippa with his own hands; now, perversely, she knew it. Not these others, not even Con with his cold, impervious eyes—Fleet.

Luke lifted his head and studied the face before him with eyes narrowed in calculation; and somewhere deep in those wary pupils a spark of hope and encouragement came to life.

" What are you getting at?" he asked cautiously.

" What I say, if you like to take the lady and light out for Holland, or wherever, what's that to me? I'm saying nothing. *Just so you don't take my money with you!* You can have your freedom and welcome, but my dough you can't have. You tell us where you've put it, and as soon as I've got it in my hands we'll all clear out of here, and leave you to put out to sea as fast as you like." He leaned a little nearer, with a wolfish smile on his lips, which were thrust out aggressively by the massive teeth within. "But if you don't act like a sensible lad, and hand over, I *will* turn you in. Better freedom without the lolly than neither a one of 'em. You think it over!"

"How do I know," demanded Luke with growing confidence, but still with some reserve, "that you'll keep your bargain? How do I know you won't take the money and then call the police on us?"

"Why should I? What have I got to gain? I came for the money, and that's all I want. And I don't need to tell you, I'm sure, that I'm not anxious to call attention to myself among the cops unless I have to. I've got to be feeling very mean to take that risk. Once I've got my money back, what have I got to feel mean about? But make no mistake, you cross me now and I can be mean as all get-out."

He got up suddenly, airily, light on his feet like so many bulky men, swung his chair back to the table, and strolled away across the room.

"Take your pick, kiddo. It's up to you."

In the momentary silence Skinner came down the stairs again, his researches completed. He spread empty hands and raised his shoulders. "Nothing up there. I left Quilley on look-out, but it's as quiet as the grave, and black as your hat on the land side. What cooks here?"

He looked from Fleet to Blackie, who was frowning in frantic thought, many coils behind in following his boss's complex proceedings; and from Blackie to Con, who had shut off what mind he had and given up the struggle some minutes ago, and was now no more than a machine for pointing a gun to order. They were all of them confounded that the hard questioning had not begun long ago. There must be a reason.

There *must* be a reason, and the reason was not any

squeamishness or compunction on Fleet's part. It was just barely possible that he really meant to withdraw once he got his hands on the money, exactly as he had said, and that he found it preferable and less messy to trade on Luke's conviction of his own guilt rather than to beat the required information out of him. But still Bunty couldn't believe it. He was more devious than that, he enjoyed being devious. There was something buried deeper, beneath this apparent reasonableness. Did he, for some obscure purpose of his own, want a Luke completely unmarked by violence? *And for what*?

"Hush!" said Fleet. "Our young friend's making up his mind. To be sensible, I hope."

"I haven't got a lot of choice, have I?" said Luke loudly; and his manner became, in some way Bunty could recognise but not define, a direct response to Fleet's, a nice balance of nervousness, doubt, and growing assurance. He had not looked at her throughout, and she understood that he dared not, that if he did his eyes would betray him, and the enemy would no longer believe in this guilt-ridden, squirming fugitive.

"It's an alternative," said Fleet, smiling at him with the first careless glint of contempt. "You can hand over and go free, or rot in gaol for fourteen years or so thinking about the money you can't get at. For a million it might be worth it—not for this little lot, not by my measure. You please yourself."

"It isn't worth it by my measure, either." He licked his dry lips and swallowed hard, reluctant but driven. "All right!" he said in a gulping breath. "You can have the damned money!"

"That's better," said Fleet warmly. "I knew you'd see sense. Where is it?"

Bunty had not the least idea what Luke was going to say. She was lost, like Fleet's henchmen, she could only wait, and be ready to follow whatever lead events and Luke offered her.

"You ought to have known, if you'd given any thought to it," said Luke, with the feeble spleen of a defeated man scrabbling for what crumbs of dignity he can salvage. "You think we were going without it, or something, when we lit out of here down to the sea? We had the stuff down there already, of course, waiting till it was dark and we could slip away without being seen."

::   ::

"Aaaah!" breathed Fleet, and pondered in silence for a moment, his eyes narrowed upon Luke's face. It was apt, it was reasonable, it would certainly have to be tested. "Go on, tell us more. Why didn't you take off as soon as you got here?"

"Because it was nearly daylight. Anybody round here would know the boat. Even if they didn't start investigating us, they might very well take it for granted the Alports were up here, and the local shop might send in, even on a Sunday, to see if they wanted supplies. There's no telephone here, people *come*. The Alports are good customers, and well known. We didn't want anyone poking around here and finding us instead, and that car in the garage. It seemed better to risk lying low to-day, and setting out after dark."

"But you put the cash aboard in advance! Then why not your luggage, too?" demanded Fleet shrewdly.

"We wanted it. Damn it, we'd been up all night, we needed a bath . . . I had to shave . . . We weren't *expecting* any trouble. I've been here before with the owners, I could account for being here if I *had* to—for everything except Pippa and the money." He wiped his forehead feverishly; there was no need to act, sweat stood on him in globules, bitter as gall on his lips. "Pippa—it was too light to risk being seen carrying her down to the boat, and anyhow, there was no way of hiding her there any better than here. No use trying to sink her here, inshore. She *had* to wait for dark. But the money, just a flat parcel, that was only a minute's job, so we made sure of it."

"It occurs to me," said Fleet thoughtfully, "that with all this talk of 'our' luggage your lady friend here doesn't seem to have any belongings, beyond a handbag—I take it that grey one belongs to her? That was going to be a bit awkward, wasn't it, girl? Are you always so improvident?"

"I've got nothing but a handbag," Bunty said with hard deliberation, "because I walked out with nothing but a handbag. Why, is my business. *He* doesn't know the reason, and you're not interested, either. He told you, he picked me up in a pub. What's the odds? If you know anything about that kid upstairs, you know that king-size case of hers is full of brand-new stuff. I carry a few extra pounds, but we're much the same size. I could get by."

Amazed, she watched the image she was projecting emerge and parade before him, no predictable bar-fly, but a woman on the dangerous verge of middle-age, a woman who had suddenly rebelled, looked over her shoulder and cut her losses. And how far from the truth was that picture? There had been a time, only twenty-four hours ago, when it would have seemed to her as close as a mirror-image. Now it was clear that she and this imaginary creature were at opposite poles, and never could, by any miracle, have touched fingertips. Fleet's eyes went over her with mild curiosity, and looked away again. To him it was a reasonably convincing portrait she had drawn, or perhaps he didn't care enough to probe any further.

"So you hid the money ready," he said, eyeing Luke, "in the boat."

"I didn't say it was in the boat." That would have been too easy, one man could go over the whole craft in ten minutes, and Luke wanted at least two of them out of the way. "It was getting light, we couldn't hang around to unlock the boat-house. We had the stuff all proofed up for sea, in oiled silk and plastic, we just fastened a nylon line on the parcel and let it down over the edge of the jetty, into the water. There's an old mooring ring down there, right at the seaward end, well down the stone facing, it'll be under water now. But you can reach it, all right, if you lie on your stomach and reach over. The end of the line's made fast to that."

Blackie Crowe had paled with shock at the thought of fifteen thousand pounds bubbling about beneath the tide on the end of a nylon line. Even Fleet's thick eyebrows arched as high as the Neanderthal bone-structure within would let them.

"I hope for your sake you *did* make it fast," he said grimly. "How come, is it weighted, then?"

Luke nodded. "Enough to keep it down out of sight." He came to his feet, slowly and cautiously, in order not to provoke Con's jumpy trigger-finger, but readily enough to show his willingness to oblige. "I'll go down with your man and show him," he said, in a soft voice that did its best not to seem too eager.

"Ah, now, just a minute, not too fast." Fleet waved him down again, but Luke, though he stayed where he was, remained standing. "How do I know you're not in Channel class in the water? You might make a break for it with a nice clean dive while one of the boys was fishing off the end of the jetty. You might even stick a toe under him and help *him* into the water. And we might still be whistling for that money. Oh, no, laddie, you won't do any showing, only on paper. We might never see you again."

Luke jerked his head at Bunty. "You'd have her, wouldn't you?" he said, aggrieved; but the very faint, opportunist glint in his eye was not quite concealed. "Think I'd do a thing like that to her?"

"Since you ask me, yes, I think you would. I'm not so sure you put the right value on the lady. No, you'll stay here."

"One man alone won't have an easy job finding it," Luke urged earnestly. "It's pitch dark down there now, he'll need somebody to give him a light, and hang on to him while he leans over. The ring must be eighteen inches

under by now, and there's a tidy drag below those rocks.
You could lose him and the money."

Fleet hesitated. "Know what, kid? I think you're
trying to pull something. You didn't have much trouble
putting it there, seemingly."

"I didn't have *any*! It was nearly daylight, and low
tide, and I know the place. It's a different cup of tea now,
for somebody who doesn't. Better let me go. I'll do the
fishing, if that'll satisfy you."

He made the offer with a tight, strained urgency and
fevered eyes, sure now that it would be refused, and sure
that he could get two of the enemy out of the house on
this fools' errand. He ventured one brief flicker of his eyes
in Bunty's direction; she knew, she was on his heels now,
close and eager.

Fleet made up his mind. It might be true, and it would
take no more than a quarter of an hour or so to put it to
the test.

"Here, come to the desk. Draw me a map, and make
it good. Direction and distance from the foot of this path
you talk about—the lot." He watched Luke stoop to rum-
mage in the top drawer of the desk for pen and writing-
pad, tear off the top sheet of the pad, and without hesitation begin to sketch in the jetty and the approach angle of
the cliff path. Satisfied, Fleet turned to Skinner, who was
lounging against the wall by the door, one shoulder
hunched as a prop. "You go down and fish up this parcel.
Take Con with you. And give me that Colt, just in case."

For one moment his back was turned squarely on Luke,
and his bulk partly hid the desk from the eyes of the others.
For once Luke could move a hand in the shelter of his own
body, and not be observed. The large, smooth granite
pebble, veined and beautiful, that his friends used as a
paperweight, lay close to his right sleeve. He closed his
hand over it and drew it towards him, sliding it quickly
into the pocket of his coat. By the time Fleet swung round
on him again he was scribbling measurements on his sketch-

map, and turned to show his hands otherwise empty and innocent as he handed it over.

"There you are. X marks the spot where the treasure's buried."

He stayed where he was as they examined it, his back to the desk. It was a good place, if they'd let him keep it. It meant that when the moment came he could draw the two remaining armed men to this side of the room to deal with him, and leave Bunty a clear run to the doorway. The lame man upstairs, edging anxiously and audibly from front window to rear window and back again, would never get down the stairs in time to intercept her.

"Seems straightforward enough," said Skinner, memorising the lay-out. "Better get that big torch out of the Riley, Con, this one here's giving out."

Without a gun in them, Con's hands were discontented and at a loss what to do with themselves. Only the weight and solidity of the Colt had held them still. They had the twitches now. Maybe Con was already hooked on one of the hard drugs, maybe he was only half-way there on LSD. Fleet himself was watching him, as the boy left the room, with a considering coldness, a practical speculation. Con might not last very long in Fleet's employ; but he hadn't become a liability yet.

Luke strained his ears for the sound of the front door opening and closing on Con's exit, opening and closing again as he came back with a large, rubber-cased torch. The latch clicked into place lightly on his return, and he came on without any delay into the living-room. The bolts were not shot, the lock no longer functioned; the way out was open.

"And who," Fleet asked suddenly, settling back in his chair, "has got the other gun—*his* gun?"

Skinner turned in the kitchen doorway. "I have. Want it?"

"Yes, hand it over." Fleet laid down the Colt close beside him on the edge of the table, and took Pippa's Lili-

put in his hands. No doubt he had supplied it in the
first place, while he still half-trusted her. "That's all. Go
on, get on with it."

Then there were four of them left in the room. They
heard the receding footsteps cross the kitchen, heard the
outer door open and close, and for a moment or two faint
sounds still reached them, dropping away down the first
steps of the path. Bunty sat erect and rigid, her eyes fixed
on Fleet. Luke quietly turned the chair round from the
desk and sat down there; and no one ordered him back to
join Bunty in the window embrasure. So much gained.
Two ways to aim and shoot now, instead of one.

Fleet had pulled a handful of paper tissues from his
pocket, and was polishing idly at the Liliput, his hands at
work almost absent-mindedly, filling in time by getting on
with the next job while he waited. His eyes studied Luke
thoughtfully across the room, with the detached assurance
of a practised mathematician solving a routine problem.

*Or an experienced undertaker measuring a potential
client for his coffin?*

Bunty had been watching the active fingers for several
seconds before their movements abruptly clicked into focus
for her, and made blinding sense. Her heart lurched and
turned in her with the shock of realisation. Suddenly she
knew what had been lying there all the while beneath the
surface manœuvrings of that tortuous mind, she knew what
kind of bargain it was that Fleet had struck with his
prisoners, and why he wanted Luke unbruised and un-
battered. Once he got his hands on the money the whole
gang would pack up and get out of here, yes; but not until
they'd staged a second and less fallible tableau for the
police to discover when they finally caught up. A murdered
girl upstairs, a girl who would eventually be traced back to
Comerbourne; in the garage the car for which the Midshire police had been putting out calls all day; and down
here in the living-room another victim, some woman the
fugitive had picked up in his flight, perhaps intending to

escape abroad with her, only to despair and put an end
to her here, before—last act of all—putting a bullet
through his own head and dying beside her. The experts
would easily demonstrate that the same gun had killed all
three, the gun the police would find in dead Luke Tennant's grip when they came. There would be no other
prints on it but his; those softly polishing fingers were
busy making sure of that now. She watched them in fascination. They had already finished with the barrel, wiped
the grip clean, taken care of the trigger-guard, and now
they were twisting another tissue neatly about the butt.

There remained only the trigger. There was no point in
wiping that, of course; not until afterwards.

CHAPTER XII

So NOW SHE KNEW the score, whether Luke knew it or not,
and they had nothing left to lose. She had perhaps two
minutes or so to make up her mind. When he starts something, she asked herself, do I run or don't I? Things are
changed now, this is a life and death matter whatever I do.
Have we a chance of getting out of here together? She
considered that with the searching eye of one who has been
through death once already, and is no longer flustered by
its proximity, and told herself with detachment that the
answer must be no. And if I run, have I a sporting chance
of getting clear alone? Yes, I believe I might have. But
have I any chance at all of reaching the police, or any
other reliable help, and bringing them back here in time to
save Luke? Over that she hesitated, but in the end the
answer was that it might be betting against the odds, but
it still might come off. With one of the victims lost, with
a witness at large who could identify them, they might
scrap the whole plan and think it wisest to get out, leave
Luke alive, and cut their losses.

Do I run, then? Yes, she told herself, I run. On balance it seems the sanest thing to do, for both of us.

There were snags, of course, in Fleet's design, but he couldn't be expected to know about all of them, and in any case he would take the small risk involved as a natural gamble. There was the broken lock on the front door. Presumably his plan envisaged that break-in as being attributed to Luke on the run; he didn't know that the key had its hiding-place right there on the spot, and that Luke was admitted to the secret, and had no need to break locks. The Alports would testify to that, and the point might stick in some Scots policeman's craw, like a husk in porridge, and refuse to be dislodged. She knew it would have stuck in George's. The shadow of the unknown other person would be there to be found, once the possibility was acknowledged. It is very difficult to erase yourself completely from the scene where you have once been, the imprint of your presence and your acts remains as a faint outline still, an indentation, never entirely smoothed out.

She wondered, for one broken instant, whether it was worthwhile calling Fleet's attention to all the discrepancies he couldn't possibly trim into his pattern. But that was no use; he didn't expect a hundred per cent perfection, perhaps he wouldn't even be happy without the residue of risk. Certainly he wouldn't be deterred by it. No, there was nothing to be done here. What she had to do was be ready to seize the moment if it came, and make sure of getting through the doorway and into the trees.

It couldn't be long now. She had done all the thinking she could do in approximately twenty seconds, though it had seemed an age. Now she rebelled at the silence. Nothing had a chance of happening successfully in this still, charged air; with a wind blowing through it there might be more hope.

"Do you mind if I have my handbag?" she said acidly, her bright stare hard and steady on Fleet's face. "You guessed right, the grey one is mine. Your fellows have had everything out of it but the lining, so don't be afraid I've got a bomb in it."

It frees the tongue, knowing that what you say will make no difference, that buttering up the devil isn't going to get you anywhere, and damning him to his face can't do more than destroy you. Something else was stirring in the unexplored depths of her being, something never yet exercised in the serenity of family life, a pure personal fury that this man and his hangers-on should take it so insultingly for granted that no one could do anything against them, that guns called tunes, that lives were expendable like draughts in a game, and their proprietors would go quietly as lambs to the slaughter, just because the odds were against them. She cast one glance at Luke, and he was waiting for it with eyes flaring wide and aware. They conversed briefly, and were at one. Neither of them knew who was going to precipitate what was coming; both of them were playing by ear. But they understood the one weapon they had, their absolute unanimity. Whichever called, the other would respond; and they had no reservations, they trusted each other through and through. It was almost worth dying for that.

"*Did* you vet it?" asked Fleet lazily, without condescending to glance either at Bunty, who had addressed him, or at Blackie, whom he was now addressing.

"Yeah, there's nothing, just women's stuff."

"I need a handkerchief," said Bunty. "Not to weep into, in case that's what you're thinking. To blow my nose. There's a smell in here. Queer, that, it was all right until you people arrived."

"Give her her bag," said Fleet, half-bored and half-amused.

It was on the bookcase, cheek by jowl with the sumptuous cream-coloured concoction Pippa had affected; and Blackie was sitting sprawled all over a high-backed chair close beside the bookcase, with Bunty diagonally to his left, and Luke diagonally to his right. He had his gun braced ready in his right hand, but his left was free to reach for the bag and toss it to Bunty. He did so, lazily and inefficiently, as if under protest.

It was a disdainful cast, an insult in itself, designed to fall short and make her stoop for her belongings. She could have caught the bag if she had cared to lean forward and stretch out her arms. Instead she sat with a straight back and a scornful face, her lips curled in detestation, and never moved a finger, but let it fall, with a dull plop and a rattle of small feminine arms within, just a yard from her feet. It lay innocently on one end of Louise Alport's most beautiful rug, a Scandinavian piece in broken forms and muted colours. A long rug, it was; the other end reposed under Fleet's hand-made shoe and Fleet's wicker chair, tilted back lazily on its rear legs beside the table.

She looked down at the bag with a fine, considering smile, and her eyes travelled the length of the rug slowly, and measured the distance to the door, and the half-way mark in that five-yard journey, the console record player with the single brass candlestick and the Benares ashtray on top of it. Her eyebrows signalled amused disdain.

"I perceive," she said, "that I am in the company of gentlemen. That's always so satisfying." And she leaned forward without haste, and stretched out a languid hand towards her property.

She moved slowly, because their eyes were too intently fixed upon her movements, she had to give Luke time for his own diversion; and as though she had whispered in his ear, he provided her with what she needed. He rose abruptly from his chair, whirled it about under the knee-hole of the desk, and took two rapid steps forward towards the bag, as if to pick it up and hand it to her, exasperated by his own impotence and their boorishness.

Attention swung upon him in an instant. Fleet dropped Pippa's gun upon the table at his elbow, and picked up the Colt with the smoothness of a snake uncoiling. Blackie's thin, sharp profile swung towards Bunty, the gun in his hand levelled and pointed, freezing upon Luke's middle. Bunty said in a high, clear voice: " Don't bother! I can stoop to conquer!"

She leaned from her place, both hands reaching for the handbag; but what she grasped, fingers clenched deep into the blessed long woollen pile, was the edge of the Scandinavian rug.

She tugged with all her heart and soul and venom and love. The rug surged across Louise Alport's polished woodblock floor like a live thing, plucking the rear legs of Fleet's chair irresistibly after it, an enthusiastic Sealyham tangling its boss in its lead and bringing him down with a shattering crash on his back.

The wicker chair screeched like a parrot, Fleet went over in a backward dive on his heavy shoulders, and his head hit the parquet with a most satisfying crunch. Attention swung back to Bunty like mad magic, and Blackie came out of his chair in a frantic leap, hesitant whether to pounce upon her, fire at her, or rush to salvage his boss. For one instant no one had time to spare for Luke, and though it was only an instant, it was enough. He plucked the granite paperweight out of his pocket, and hurled it into the light fixture with all his might—he had played cricket for his school and college as a fast bowler of erratic speed but deadly accuracy.

To Bunty, swept suddenly away out of reach of fear on a wave of exultant battle-madness that stemmed from somewhere very far back in her ancestry, the sequence of events was for ever crystal clear, though they all followed one another so rapidly as to be virtually simultaneous. The first thing was that Fleet was on his back, but still with the Colt in his hand, and all his resilient faculties gathering in his trigger-finger. The next was that she was on her feet, hands stretched up to the extreme of her reach, flourishing the rug. It was interposed between her body and the gunmen for an instant too brief to measure, but in its shelter she flung herself to one side, expecting the shot

that would surely come. It came from Blackie, though
she would have bet on Fleet. Fleet was always to surprise
her. Even on his back, balance gone and senses momentarily disorientated, he made an instant decision, and it was
at Luke he fired. The two shots stuttered like a double
report, but between the two Bunty, hardly aware whether
she was intact or not, had done the beautifully simple
thing, and hurled the rug from her, to descend with all
its woolly suffocation over the sprawling figure on the floor.
Fleet's shot, blanketed by Swedish blues and greens, foils
to all that orange and white, burned a hole in the rug and
went wild, plunking harmlessly into the wall.

And only then did Luke's pebble hit the glowing fluorescent ring in the middle of the ceiling, hard and accurately
at the point where the glass fitted into its plastic seal. A
loud note of song, almost too high to be within human
range, vibrated above their heads. There was a spitting explosion of brilliant, bluish radiance, like close lightning,
and then a darkness like midnight and heavy rain, absolute
darkness coruscating with piercing, infinitesimal points of
sound, a rain of bitter ice. Fine particles of glass whispered
down into hair and eyelids and folds of clothing. And on
the instant all the lights in the house went out.

In a darkness which he could navigate only from
memory, Luke took a flying leap, and came down heavily
with both feet on the threshing canvas backing of the Scandinavian rug. He had aimed for where he hoped Fleet's
solar plexus would be, but no part of Fleet was ever going
to be where one expected to find it. Nothing else so big
could ever have been so elusive. He had foreseen the line
of attack, and rolled himself under the table, swinging clear
of the mouthfuls of exquisitely-dyed long-pile wool that had
threatened to smother him. From under the table he lunged
in a round swipe, found Luke's left foot, and gripped like
an octopus. Luke lifted his right foot, and stamped it down
with all his weight on the wrist of the hand that held him.
There were no rules. He hadn't even known, until he

began, whether he could fight or not. He had never fought since he was about ten years old. He wanted to cry out to Bunty to run, but he dared not, for fear one of the enemy should divert his attention to her in time. Surely, surely she would take her chance now, as he had begged her.

And Bunty had meant to; but it must have been out of some misconception of what she was, for things turned out quite differently. She launched herself towards the doorway, made a long controlled sweep of her left hand along the wall, and found the brass candlestick on top of the record player. The rounded candle-holder fitted snugly into her hand. She gripped it firmly, even took time to settle it comfortably. There seemed to be no haste, the gale that carried her accommodated itself to the speed of events, and made everything seem easy and leisurely, as though these happenings took their time from her, and not she from them. She paced out without hindrance the remaining yards to the door, seized the handle and hurled the door wide open, so that the wooden panels shuddered against the rubber door-stop. But when she ran, it was because the darkness was already beginning to pale for her, and the direction in which she ran was back into the room, towards the shapeless mêlée in the twilight there. She did not think at all, except with her blood and her bones. Bunty had lost herself in the gale-force wind of her own instincts, which had never been loose like this before, and probably never would be again.

Fleet's long arm heaved convulsively under Luke's foot, and a grunting curse jerked from under the uncurling edge of the rug. Then the right hand that held the Colt hooked itself round Luke's knees and brought him down in a crashing fall on top of his adversary. The moment of alarm was already over, and Fleet still wanted him alive, and if possible undamaged. A suicide should not have the grazes and bruises of a stand-up fight all over him, it tends to complicate the proceedings of the coroner's court. Bunty, one hand extended to catch at Luke's sleeve and guide him to the doorway, had a precarious hold on him when he fell, but the fall dragged him out of her grasp. She circled the two threshing bodies on the floor, and could not distinguish friend from enemy. But the third presence, still erect, was now visible as her eyes grew accustomed to the darkness. Blackie, too, was circling the wrestlers, and probing forward into the untidy struggle with his gun hand. And Blackie was not in his master's secrets, and by the shape and the movement and the long, steady, hissing breath of him he meant to shoot the instant the chance offered.

A head and shoulders reared out of the tangle on the floor. Someone got a foot to the ground and laboured to pull clear and spring erect, and by the slightness and shape of the shadow emerging from shadows Bunty knew him for Luke. So did Blackie, and took a rapid step to one side to have his target well clear of Fleet's bulk when he fired. The movement took him nearer to Bunty, who had hung for one appalled instant torn between grabbing at Luke's arm to pull him clear, and hurling herself at the weaving manikin who threatened him.

She chose Blackie. The brass candlestick, swung underhand with all her strength and fury behind it, took him fairly and squarely on the point of the right elbow. The blow had been designed only to sweep his gun hand upwards, but by luck it did much more. It hit his funny-bone with a tingling shock that paralysed him to the finger-tips. The gun was jerked out of his hand, and flew jarring across the parquet floor. He uttered a weird, sharp yelp of pain that trailed off into incoherent curses, and went groping lamely after his weapon across the floor, like a crippled spider, one arm dangling.

Bunty swung the candlestick back, startled and exhilarated by success, and struck blindly at Fleet. The blow was smothered in a thick shoulder that rolled aside and rode it almost casually, and then a hand grasped the base of her weapon and pulled dexterously and sharply to jerk her off her feet. Instinctively she released her grip and let the thing go, springing back from too close contact. And then Luke had scrambled clear and was on his feet, and had her by the hand.

"Quick . . . *run*!"

Neither of them had heard, or could possibly have heard in that chaotic interlude, the labouring footsteps dragging their way down the stairs. They had forgotten Quilley. Fleet fired after them towards the door as he came to his knees, but the bullet plugged harmlessly into the lintel. It was the other shot that stopped them cold as they hurled themselves out into the hall, a shot that spat accurately into the wood blocks of the floor just before their feet, and flung them back in a frantic recoil against the balustrade of the staircase. It came from the corner just within the front door, out of absolute darkness, whereas they had one faint light upon them from the glass panel of the door, and another behind them from the open doorway of the living-room.

"Hold it right there!" said Quilley's voice, faintly stirred this time with earnest zeal, for who was the useful one now? "I can see you, and you can't see me. One step this way and I plug you."

Luke recovered from the check in a moment, but a moment was too long. If they could not both get away, he could still break a way through for Bunty, and this time she would have to go, because there would be nothing left for her to do here, no one to salvage. He put her aside by the shoulder, flattening her into the shelter of the newel-post, and sprang for the armed darkness, diving low.

His arms found and circled Quilley's knees, Quilley's gun hand swung towards the ceiling, and down they went in an ugly, heavy fall in the corner beside the door, both heads jarred against the wall.

"*Run*, Bunty!" Luke panted, clawing his way along Quilley's right arm towards the gun, and forcing the struggling wrist to point the barrel away into the wall.

The way was clear for her to reach the door, but time

had already run out. The narrow hall was suddenly full of people. Blackie had an arm locked round Bunty's neck, and his gun pressed left-handed into her back. And Fleet was lunging past them to reach Luke and Quilley and drag them apart. A faint, flickering pencil of light suddenly sprang up, scurrying through the living-room to shed a queasy pallor on the struggle, and after it a cone of steady light from Con's long, rubber-cased torch came surging eagerly in. They were back from the jetty far too soon, and empty-handed, just in time to put the quietus on all hope of escape.

The beam of yellow light swung upwards and bounded along the ceiling, swung downwards again and danced over the glass panel of the door. The thick rubber case hit Luke low in the back of the head with a solid, sickening sound. His shoulders hunched oddly, he hung still for an instant, and then collapsed over Quilley like a discarded rag-doll, and lay in a motionless sprawl of arms and legs and lolling head, dead to the world.

::   ::

"All right," said Fleet's voice out of the dark, soft, savage and frightening, "bring them back inside. All right! There are other ways."

He was out of breath, ruffled, bruised. He looked from Luke's huddled body to his own awed and silent lieutenants; he looked at Bunty, and the ray of the torch showed her his face outlined in abrupt lights and shadows, planes of steep pallor and obliques of dusty black. All the debonair, easy, vigorous bonhomie had cracked and fallen away from those razor-edged surfaces. This was basic Fleet, the bedrock fact of what he had made of himself, for in every aspect of him Fleet was a selfmade man. Neither her life nor Luke's was worth half a crown now, but for one thing. Fleet still didn't know where the money was. And Luke was past questioning. A respite for him, at least; he'd had more than enough. Now she was left. Fleet's marmalade eyes, orange-flecked, glowed almost to red as he stared at her.

Without turning his head he addressed Quilley, who had clambered painfully to his feet again, and was holding himself up by the wall. " Get back upstairs, and keep a sharp eye out. Somebody could have heard the shots."

"Yes, sure, boss, I'm going. I had to come down . . . the front door . . . they'd have made it if I hadn't . . ." He edged away along the wall, eager and anxious, hooked an arm heavily over the bannister rail, and began to drag himself back to his guard duty. The torch caught the whites of his eyes, turned back hopefully and fearfully upon Fleet.

"All right, you had to come down! *Now get back!*"

Quilley went in fear, groaning as he climbed.

"Well, what happened to you two?" But he knew already. "There was nothing there, of course."

"Nothing. No ring, even. A lot of lies," Con said indignantly.

"We had to get out of sight fast, too," Skinner supplemented. "There's a boat making up-coast, not far offshore. We didn't want to be seen. But we'd already made sure. He was lying, all right."

"Bring him in," said Fleet, and stalked ahead of them into the living-room.

Blackie prodded Bunty before him into the ravaged room, and pushed her down into the settee. The other two dragged in Luke by his arms and tumbled him on the floor in front of her feet, a thin, long, disjointed puppet. They had only the two torches for light, the small, guttering candle that belonged to the Alports, and the illuminated club that had battered Luke into unconsciousness. Fine slivers of glass crunched under their feet, and drew thin silver-point lines the length of Luke's dangling hand.

By this curiously stagey lighting Bunty looked round the chaos of the room, from the shattered light-fixture to the door-lintel where Fleet's second bullet had buried itself.

There was no passing this off as a murder and suicide from despair now. Did that make bargaining possible? No, not a hope. There was a lot of room in the sea, and such witnesses as Fleet had at his mercy were better out of the way.

"You'll need a new script, won't you?" she heard herself saying with unbelievable calm. "Four bullet-holes to account for, and all this wreckage. And after you'd polished all the prints off the business gun, too! I can't wait to see you tidy this lot up."

"Too true," said Fleet, in a voice as soft as it was vicious. "You couldn't have put it better—*you can't wait*! You're too sharp, my dear, too sharp altogether. A lot too sharp for your own good. Wouldn't you do better to co-operate, and tell me where the money's hidden?"

"No," she said with a tight, tired smile, "I shouldn't. That's the last thing I'd be likely to do, even if I knew. You're so sure I've got no time left. But I have! I've got until you know the answer to that, either from him or from me. That long, and not many minutes longer. You think I don't know a killer when I see one? If I told you what you want to know, that *would* be the last thing I should do. So wouldn't I be a fool to tell you? *Even if I knew?*"

Fleet hit her then, with his open hand, deliberately and yet not too hard. He took pleasure in weighing and measuring the blow nicely, to jerk back her head and send a jarring shock down her spine without, as yet, doing her any damage. And Bunty laughed.

"You think you can open my mouth that way? I should have to find living more uncomfortable than dying before I'd be driven to talk. And I like living. I'll put up with a lot for it. By the time you'd got me to the amenable stage, I should be incapable of telling you anything at all. I'm not the kind that dies easily. Either way, you'll never know."

Luke, crumpled at her feet, heaved a deeper breath into him, and moaned. Ignoring the guns, Bunty slid from her place and crouched upon the parquet beside him. She lifted his head into her lap, and stroked back his lank hair. A spasm dragged his face awry for a moment, and smoothed out again into the indifference of unconsciousness.

"Boss," said Blackie in a low voice, "I reckon you'd be wasting time on her. I don't believe she knows. He'd never trust her that far. Damn it, he only picked her up last night, on the run. It's *him* we want."

She gathered the limp body more closely into her lap, arched over him jealously. Let them think that, by all means, until Luke showed signs of coming round. Until then, he was safe. There was nothing they could do to him, and nothing effective they could do to her. To keep silence might be a slow sentence of death, but to speak was instant death, and between the two there was not much doubt of her preference. Time, if it took sides at all, was on her side, hers and Luke's. Things become very simple when you have no choice, when there's nothing left for you but to endure as long as you can, and survive if you can.

"Get him round, then," Fleet spat viciously. "Pour cold water on him, anything, only bring him round, quick."

Bunty laid her hand on Luke's forehead, holding him at rest, willing him to remain absent.

"*Damn you!*" hissed Fleet through his teeth, in sudden fury, and kicked out ferociously at the limp body before him.

Bunty uttered a brief, furious cry, and flung herself across Luke's helpless form, spreading her own arm and shoulder to ward off the blow. The face that glared up at Fleet, with bared teeth and flashing eyes, was the face of the antique woman that Cæsar respected, the red-haired Celtic Amazon who emerged at need to fight shoulder to shoulder with her menfolk, huge, noble and daunting. Bunty's Welsh ancestry went back beyond the small dark men. She saw Fleet start back from her in astonishment, almost in dread, so unused was he to people who forget to

be afraid. She saw the gun in his hand prick up like a live
snake, its cold eye fending her off; and she laughed, staring it down defiantly, with Luke gathered close into her
arms from harm.

"Go ahead, then, shoot! Shoot, and then hunt for your
money till your heart bursts, and much good may it do you,
Mister Fleet!"

His mouth fell slack, he drew back from her a step in
almost superstitious recoil; and in the moment of stricken
silence they all heard Quilley's voice calling down the well
of the stairs in agitation, and trailing a hollow echo after it:

"Boss . . . boss! There's a boat-load of men coming in
towards the inlet. They've put out their lights . . . they're
coming in to land . . . !"

: :   : :

Fleet turned and rushed to the window, dragging the
curtains aside and craning to see down into the inlet, to the
faint phosphorescent glow that was the sea, palpitating and
shimmering with almost imperceptible movement. Skinner,
who was nearest to the door, made for the stairs and went
up them three at a time. Crouched on the floor with Luke
inert in her arms, Bunty heard their footsteps crossing the
boards overhead, Skinner rapid and blunt, Quilley dragging like a crippled beast, crossing and re-crossing from
front windows to rear, and back again. Con and Blackie
crowded to the window behind Fleet's hulking shoulders,
peering, straining their eyes, holding their breath.

They had forgotten her. In a moment of time everything
had gone into reverse. She could have risen and walked out
at the front door, and she felt that no one would ever have
noticed. Fear, anger and stress withdrew and stood at gaze,
distant in the dark corners of the room, still present but
now almost dreamlike, unable to touch the island where she
kneeled with Luke's heavy head in her arms. She made
no move, she said nothing, she had no conscious thoughts;
there was no longer any need for her to think or act, and

because there was no more need, suddenly she had no more power.

Distantly, like something remembered, she heard Skinner's voice calling urgently down the well of the stairs:

"Boss, they're over the other side, too . . . among the trees, five or six of 'em. . . ."

There had been no sound of a car, no glimpse of headlights. They had drawn in as silently as the night itself; so they knew what kind of hunt this was, and what to expect when they sprang the trap. Could this be all on account of Rosamund Chartley and her mythical address in Hereford?

There was a hoarse, muted shout overhead, a rush for the stairs. Skinner came bounding down in three stumbling leaps, fending himself off from walls and furniture with flailing arms.

"Boss, it's the police! We better get out of here fast . . . they're all round us. . . ."

A sudden pale eye of light stroked its way down the wall, dimmed and diffused by the drawn curtains, probing at the window and passing in absolute silence. In a moment they saw it through the open door of the living-room, spilled in a lace of pallor on the floor of the hall, patterned by the frosted glass in the front door. When it passed from there, there would be darkness across the stretch of gravel to where the Jaguar stood in the shelter of the trees, turned and ready to run.

"That's it, then," Fleet said in a clipped whisper, meant for no ears but his own, though Bunty heard it with the exaggerated clarity of voices in dreams. He knew the game was up. He knew when to throw in his hand.

The light passed on from the hall, and left the front door in darkness again.

"Now!" hissed Fleet. "*Out! Run for the Jag!*"

And out they went, tumbling, jostling, thrusting, all in something so like silence that their flight became more dreamlike than their lingering. Fleet was first out of the

door, fast and light on his feet, a man well named; and
after him Blackie, hurtling like a terrier, Con, outlined for
a moment in the doorway all arms and legs, Skinner pound-
ing along heavily in the rear and rolling like a half-filled
barrel. All the darkling crew streamed out across the open
court before the cottage, night-birds startled from their
carrion. Bunty sat dazed with all the accumulated weariness of a night and a day, and listened to their flight.

There was a postscript. Leaning heavily on the ban-
nisters, Quilley came stumbling and groaning after, down
the stairs and through the hall.

"Boss, wait for me . . . don't go without me . . . !"

She heard the moaning complaint ebb along the wall,
and reach the front door. And then the two of them were
alone. Stiffly she got up from the floor, laying Luke
gently down out of her arms, and went out into the
porch.

The sound of all those running feet on the gravel had
roused the whole garden. It was like Birnam Wood coming
to Dunsinane. Pencils of light sprang up from three points,
two among the trees on one side of the gate, one from the
rough grass on the other, and converged upon the racing
figures; and suddenly the copse began to spawn men, they
came swarming out on the run, and streamed from all
directions towards the Jaguar. They were already between
the fugitives and the Riley. A little spurt of flame stabbed
the darkness, a shot fired at the tyres, not at the men. Fleet
didn't retaliate, didn't swerve or halt or hesitate, he charged
straight for the grey car, darted round in its shelter to the
driving seat, and in a moment the engine soared into life,
and the car began to move, gathering speed like a grey-
hound out of a trap. With three of its four doors wide open
and vibrating like wings, it surged across the gravel towards the open gate, while the rest of the crew scrambled
and clawed their way aboard. He kept it idling for them a
matter of seconds only. The nearest policeman was not
ten yards away.

Quilley, last of the queue, came hobbling agonisingly after, appealing aloud in a high wail of outrage:

"Boss, wait for me . . . wait for me . . . you can't . . ."

He was hopping frantically alongside as they gathered speed; he got a grip on the front passenger door and clung in desperation.

"Give me a hand . . . Con, give me a hand . . ."

But it was Fleet who gave him a hand. They were four aboard, and wanted all the speed they could make, and no overloading. Fleet leaned across Con to the open door, spread his large palm against Quilley's chest and shoved him off, neatly catching the door as it swung loosely back, and slamming it shut. The car leaped clear of the pursuers by a matter of feet, and Quilley, hurled from his hold, fell sprawling under it.

The rear wheel heaved and lurched over his foot, the Jaguar slewed round insecurely for an instant, and then shot away through the gate and roared round the curve of the drive. Quilley's scream and the exultant tiger-purr of the acceleration died away together, diminuendo along the calm air of the night. A cluster of dark figures surrounded the rumpled heap on the ground. The light-grey Jaguar was gone along the sunken lane, hell-bent for the main road.

Suddenly it was abnormally quiet, and everything was over.

CHAPTER XIII

LUKE CAME ROUND with a skull full of hammers and a mouth full of old cobwebs, springing into instant, jangling awareness of Bunty's arm under his head and Bunty's palm cupping his cheek, and a bolt of hurtful light probing over them both out of the darkness. The edge of the falling beam showed him the end of a man's dark sleeve, and a hand holding a gun.

There was no end to it, and no escape. He set a palm

to the floor in frantic haste and levered himself up groggily
to his knees, leaning between Bunty and the threat, trying
to put her behind him, though the sudden movement set his
head ringing like a cracked bell, and the torch burned a
hole through his eyes and into his brain. And Bunty drew
him back gently into her arms and held him there, her
cheek pressed against his forehead.

"It's all right, my dear, it's all right! The police are
here. . . . It's all over, we're safe. . . ."

"Safe . . . ?" he repeated dazedly. He lifted a shaky
hand and touched her cheek. "They didn't hurt you . . . ?
Where are they?"

"They got away in the Jaguar . . . all but the lame
one. . . ."

"They'll no' get far." The darkness spoke in the voice
of the sergeant with the pepper-and-salt hair, in tones of
ripe satisfaction. The gun vanished into a jacket pocket.
The torch settled briefly upon Bunty's pale, soiled face,
and considerately turned its beam aside. "We've got a
road-block up in the cutting. They'll no' get through that.
You're all right, ma'am?"

She nodded: now that the tension was broken she was
almost too tired to speak.

"And your right name, now," he asked cautiously. "It
wouldn't be Felse, would it?"

"Yes," she said, "I'm Bunty Felse."

"Thank God for that!" said the sergeant with profound
satisfaction, and in all innocence kicked away the newly-
recovered world from under Luke's feet. "Your husband's
been going daft, worrying about you."

: :   : :

How strange, how very strange, that it had never even
occurred to him to think that she might belong to someone else! As if such a woman as she was could ever have
come so far through life without being recognised, desired,
loved. She had seemed to belong so surely to him, to be a
miracle created specially for his salvation, without any

existence previous to their meeting. But of course she was flesh and blood, like ordinary women. For him she had no age, no class, no kin, there had been nothing before he found her. But of course she had known all those years of her life without him, before ever he existed for her. She had known a marriage, and a husband who was going daft, worrying about her.

Luke lay very still, overwhelmed with the magnitude of his desolation and loss. And what confounded him most was the paradox of being in her arms, linked with her in an alliance such as surely she had never in her life experienced with any man before, or ever would with any man after. He both possessed and had lost her.

::   ::

Three men came in from the seaward side, and one more from the landward, and this last was an inspector, no less. They found candles in one of the kitchen cupboards, and the young constable of the morning, taciturn as ever, rummaged among Reggie Alport's electrical spares and did some minor miracles with fuse-wire. Soon he had the current working in the kitchen, at least, so that they could do a little preliminary first-aid on Quilley before the ambulance came. The door stood open between the kitchen and the living-room, to share the benefit of the light.

" No," admitted the inspector ruefully, " I'm afraid we didn't check up on your fictional Mrs. Chartley at first. I only wish we had, we should have been here earlier. But you seemed all above-board to McCabe, and we had no reason then to be looking out for a woman. No, what put us on to you was further information from your home county. You can thank your son for it, indirectly. It seems he came home without notice late on Saturday evening, and found nobody there to welcome him. When nobody came back by eleven he called your husband's chief, and found that Mr. Felse had gone down south on a job, so he naturally took it for granted you might have decided to travel with him for the ride. It wasn't until some child turned up next morning, saying she'd found your purse, that he began to wonder."

All the threads were beginning to tie in neatly into the pattern, even some of which the police would never know anything. So that was why there'd been no letter from Dominic, because he intended to rush home in person for her birthday, and surprise her. And if he'd been a couple of hours earlier, perhaps she would never have gone out walking to shake off her demon, never entered " The Constellation Orion," never met Luke Tennant. And perhaps, when he was at the end of his tether, Luke Tennant would have given up thinking of Norway, and pointed that little gun at his temple and pulled the trigger, as he had so nearly done when the police came knocking at the door.

" So he told your C.I.D. chief, and they got in touch with your husband, and nobody knew where you were, or why you should be missing. Then they really began hunting. And it seems there's an old chap who saw you late on Saturday night with a young man he didn't know, and was sufficiently nosy to take note of the car and its number."

" Old Lennie," she said, and smiled. " We bought some coffee at his stall. Thank God for nosy people! I see! So then they added my description to the information about NAQ 788, and circulated it. And Mrs. Chartley filled the bill well enough to be worth investigating. And you found the Alports had never heard of her, and her address didn't exist."

" That's about it. So we thought it best to move in on you here pretty cautiously. We felt you must have been under duress this morning when you answered the door. A loaded gun a yard or so from your back can turn anybody into a first-class dissembler. It was the only way we could account for your behaviour."

" I know," she admitted, " my behaviour throughout has been far from what you'd expect of a policeman's wife.

But there's more to this than a couple of traffic offences. They haven't said anything to you about a murder?"

They hadn't. Nor, it seemed, about the snatching of Armitage Pressings' weekly pay-roll. Apparently nobody had missed Pippa Gallier yet, and no one suspected the connection between these events scattered through two months of time and three hundred miles or so of country. Bunty and Luke had still quite a lot to account for. The dead girl upstairs was going to come as a shock. And the money . . .

Bunty had almost forgotten about the money, but it was high time to retrieve it now. It was, after all, the chief evidence they had to offer for their own integrity, and the stake for which they had defied Fleet and all his private army.

"Before we start," she said, "could you send one of your men down to the jetty to fetch something? Something I hid there. A flat parcel in gift-wrapping paper." She turned her head and looked at Luke, sitting drained and pale and sad beside her. "It's under one of the slabs of slate that form the steps, only about three yards up from the jetty," she said, for Luke rather than for anyone else. "I pushed it under there when I slipped and fell. If you hadn't been solidly between Quilley and me I could never have got away with it, even in the dark."

The inspector looked at the raw-boned young constable who was good with fuses, and the constable, whose ears, like his eyes, missed nothing, took one of the torches without a word, and went off through the kitchen to the cliff path.

"And exactly what," asked the inspector curiously, "is in this gift parcel? What has it got to do with this business?"

"Everything," she said simply. "It's what those men were after, it's what they killed the girl for—the girl upstairs—not to speak of the man who was driving the van when they snatched it in the first place. It's a week's pay-roll from a big firm outside Comerbourne. Getting on for fifteen thousand pounds in notes."

"I think," said the inspector carefully, after a pause to regain his breath, "you'd better tell me the whole story."

Between the two of them they told him. By the time they were half-way through, the recital was punctuated by Quilley's first half-conscious moans from the kitchen, and the inspector was unrolling the parcel of notes on the table before him. The sound of police cars halting before the door of the cottage put in the final full-stop. Fleet and his lieutenants were back under guard.

A hefty red-headed sergeant came in first from the night, his arms full of guns and his face one broad, freckled beam of fulfilment.

"Regular arsenal, sir . . . four of 'em!" He laid them out proudly on the table before his chief, and for an instant his jaw dropped at sight of the treasure already deployed there. "Two revolvers, nice brand-new Colt Agent and a German Pickert .32. A Webley and Scott .25 automatic . . . and this little squib . . . that's another German job, a Menz Liliput. Wouldn't think that could do any damage, would you?"

The inspector viewed them without noticeable enthusiasm. Guns had never figured in the crimes that came within his ordinary range, and to him, as to George in Comerbourne, they were an omen of times changing for the worse. He looked up at Luke over the array of armaments.

"Which one?"

"The one you're holding." The Webley was almost as tiny, but he would have known that Liliput again among thousands, by the associations that clung to it, by Bunty's confiding presence at his side, by the memory of that ride in which he could hardly believe now, when this little ugly shape had bound her into stillness and submission, who now sat beside him as an ally of her own will, held by nothing but her own generosity and loyalty. At every mention of her husband and son, those two who had genuine rights in her, the pain in his heart had tightened and intensified by one more turn. But still, every now and again, she spoke for both of them, and said " we," and all that tension was released each time she said it, and he knew that she was not lost to him, that she was indeed, in some measure, his, and his for life.

" You realise, of course," said the inspector gently, for he was a man of intuition as well as intelligence, and had already placed his own stake, " that he's sure to have alibis for everything?"

" Yes, I know. I don't care now. If you want to hold me, that's all right. I'm satisfied now."

" What happened?" asked the inspector, folding the gay paper over the indecent display of wealth, and looking up at the sergeant.

" They tried to crash the barrier. Bent that nice grey paint job badly, stove her nose right in. They poured out in all directions when she stalled, but we got 'em all fielded in quick time. They didn't fire. Soon as we laid hands on 'em they started acting legal. They hadn't done anything, they were on their lawful occasions. Only the big chap talks."

" Yes," said the inspector resignedly, " only he would. Still, better bring 'em in until the wagon arrives."

Fleet came in with rock-like assurance, his hands in his pockets, his henchmen mute and stolid behind him. And of course they would all have a dozen witnesses to testify that they had been somewhere miles away when the Armitage pay-roll was snatched, and at least outside the house when Pippa Gallier was shot; and of course they would even have licences for all those guns, except Pippa's, of which they would deny all knowledge prior to yesterday. And of course, regarding the money and their presence here, and their flight when the police came, Fleet would tell the same old story of being robbed by Pippa, of actually breaking in on Luke's house to find Pippa dead and

Luke drunk and unconscious, of pursuing Luke here into
Scotland after the money—with some mildly illegal origin
for the money, something almost innocuous, but enough to
account for a certain shyness of the police. . . .

Yes, it was all implicit in his bearing as he came in.

: :   : :

"Keys?" said Fleet, smiling, always smiling, with deep-
sunk marmalade eyes mildly indignant, but no more, with
salient bones grown bland with tolerance under the tanned
and gleaming skin, a benevolent, misjudged man. "What
should I know about her keys? I expect he threw 'em
away. *I* never saw any such little leather boot. You can
search me." Which of course they could, and any residence
of his into the bargain; he wasn't such a fool as to keep a
thing so easily identifiable.

"Look, I've told you that money was ours, and it's got
nothing to do with any pay-roll, it's racing winnings. We
had a syndicate. And a system. You fellows wouldn't ap-
prove, but you'd have a job to pick us up on it, all the
same, I'm telling you that. Naturally we came after it.
What would you have done, written it off? More fool me,
for ever letting that little bitch hold the kitty, but she had
a way with her. . . . Ask *him*, *he* knows! She double-
crossed him, too, and he paid her her dues, and good luck
to him. But don't look at *me*! I can prove where I was all
the early part of Saturday evening. By the time I got there
it was all over.

"And that's all I am saying," said Fleet, still beneficently
smiling. "I want to see my lawyer before I say another
word."

"And you've got licences for all these cannon, I suppose?" said the inspector, mildly shuffling Pippa's passport and air ticket in his hands. The bone-cased eyes lin-
gered on them hungrily, but gave nothing away. There was
something else there, too, sandwiched between the two
documents, something Bunty and Luke hadn't discovered
because it was slim enough and small enough to hide among

the notes: a sealed white envelope, stamped, ready for the post.

"One of 'em's nothing to do with me, ask *him* about that. For mine I have. All but the Pickert, maybe. I picked that up during the war. It's damned hard to keep within the law *all* the time," said Fleet tolerantly.

"But you deny playing any part in Pippa Gallier's death? Or in the wage-snatch from Armitage Pressings?" The inspector slipped the point of his ball-pen almost absent-mindedly inside the flap of the envelope, and began to slide it along. It was noticeable that he did not touch the envelope itself, but held it between passport and ticket; and the address had appeared for a moment to engage more of his attention than he was actually giving to Fleet.

"That I don't mind repeating. I followed her to this chap's place, I got kind of restless waiting for her to come out, and I went in to find out what was happening. She was on the floor, dead, and this young fellow was out cold on the top of her, with the gun in his hand. And if he didn't shoot her, then get on with finding out who did, because you won't get anywhere looking at me. Two of my lads were with me, they know she was dead when we went in. That's it!" said Fleet, with a snap of his formidable jaws like a shark bisecting an unlucky bather. "I've finished talking."

"*But I haven't!*" snarled a sudden ferocious voice from the kitchen. "*I'm just set to begin.*"

::   ::

As one man they swung to face the doorway. The voice was one they had none of them heard before, though several of them had heard the same man speak. Fleet knew this voice muted, anxious and willing to please, Luke knew it injured, whining and doomed, aware of its narrowing destiny. The police had heard it only in one wild scream as the car went over its protests, and flattened them into the gravel.

Propped on a policeman's arm, Quilley leaned from

the kitchen rug, his left leg stripped from the knee down, his foot crushed and leaning disjointedly sidewise from the ankle. By straining to the limit of his strength he could just get his eyes upon Fleet, and they aimed there like gun-barrels, as deadly and as fixed. He was not afraid now, he had nothing to lose, he could close the doors on the man who had tyrannised over him, and if he closed them on himself, too, that would still be liberation. Fleet had tossed him to the police like a bone to hounds, to delay the pursuit. There was a price for that.

"Here's one," said Quilley stridently, "who wants to talk, and he's got plenty to tell, too. Of course that's the Armitage money, and I was there when we snatched it, and what you want to know about that I can tell you, *even who fired the shot*. But it wasn't *him*, not that time. He hasn't got the guts to go out and do a job, he just directs from a safe place. It was the girl he killed . . . with his own hands . . . and I was there to see it. . . ."

For one moment it seemed that Fleet would hurl himself. out of his chair, clean through all opposition, and clamp his hands round Quilley's throat. But he did not. He sat back by a cautious inch or two in his seat, to demonstrate how little this attack meant to him; and his face with all its death's-head boniness continued to smile.

"It was after she asked for the gun," Quilley pursued loudly and firmly, "that he got uneasy. She was getting above herself, and his women don't do that. But he still fancied her, then, so he gave her a gun of sorts to keep her happy—that rubbishing little thing you've got there, the one he's trying to kid you is nothing to do with him. . . ."

"That?" said Fleet blankly, wide-eyed in innocence. "I never saw the thing in my life until yesterday."

"Like hell he never saw it! He gave it to her. He was never too sure about her after that, but when he slept with her Friday night he took a peep at the case with the money in it, and it looked all right. But still his thumbs pricked about her, so he had us watch her, see what she'd do. And Saturday night, after she thought he'd gone back to town, she came bustling out with a suitcase, and locked her flat, and went off in a taxi, so we had to notify him. Con and Blackie followed her in the Riley, while I waited for *him*, and he let us into her flat to make sure about the money. He didn't need her keys for that, he'd had one made for himself long ago, but she didn't know that. You think he'd leave any money of his behind a door he couldn't get through when he liked? And what do you know? She'd filled the case up with bundles of newspaper cuttings, only the top note in each clip was real. So then he knew she was off with the dough. They had orders to pick her up and bring her back if she tried to run out by train, or anything, but she never, she went to this little house, and walked right in, so they called him at her flat, and we went over there fast. The door wasn't locked, it was easy. We walked in, and there she was waving this gun at this kid, and raving how he'd got to keep his promise to her, and he went for her as if he thought it was a pop-gun, he was so tight, and there they were fighting for it, and *him* in the doorway weighing it all up, like he always does everything, *what's in it for Fleet*! And *I*," said Quilley vengefully, "*I* was the one who was right there beside him. I saw him club this kid cold. Nobody knows how to do it better. I saw him take the gun out of his hand. And she, she was all over him suddenly, she says, darling, she says, thank heaven you came, she says, he'd have killed me! And there she is hanging round Fleet's neck, hoping he's only just busted in, and he puts that gun to her chest and shoots her dead. Just like that!"

"Poor devil!" said Fleet, with hardly a pretence at sincerity. "Hysterical. He's got it in for me, I always knew he hated my guts. He'll say anything."

"Not anything, just the facts, Fleet. Nobody needs more. I tell you, he shot her. And then he wiped the gun and put it back in the kid's hand, and arranged the two of 'em there, all ready to be found, so the kid could take the rap. We called the cops from a call box to come and get him, only he must have come round too soon and cleared out. And there's one thing I can tell you, too. She'd been getting ready to put the finger on the lot of us, and especially Fleet. In her flat we found some trial runs for a letter she was putting together for the police, all cut out of newspapers, half a dozen different types. She was headed out, and she was going to make good and sure we wouldn't be at large to hunt for her. Oh, yes, we went back to her flat . . . just as soon as we found there was no money in her suitcase and nothing in her bag, no left-luggage ticket, or anything like that. We took her keys and went back to turn the whole place out, but all we found was these bits of paper, where she'd been experimenting with this letter. About the Armitage job, and about Pope Halsey's furs, too. She knew all about that, she was the one who tipped us off about the shipment. We had a proper hunt, but we never found anything else, and he burned those bits of paper. Anything you want to know," said Quilley, incandescent with vengeance, " you ask me. I was there every time, there's nothing I can't tell you."

" Nothing," said Fleet, crossing one grey-worsted leg negligently over the other, and grinned towards the kitchen doorway, round which the frantic eyes glared and gloated on him. " And nothing he won't, either, true or false. You can see he'd do anything to knife me in the back. But I've got witnesses will prove the opposite . . . witnesses with nothing to gain."

" *Except money*!" said Quilley. " Alibis he gets wholesale."

"You see?" said Fleet, sighing. "Poor chap! Psychopathic, really!"

"Then you didn't go back to her flat?" asked the inspector mildly.

"Who said we didn't? She'd run out with my money . . . *our* money . . . we didn't know what she'd done with it. . . ."

"And he couldn't ask her," said Quilley viciously. "He was too sure it would be there in her suitcase, he'd fired first and looked afterwards."

"Of course we went back to look in her flat, where else was it likely to be? But we didn't find any trial shots at synthetic letters to the police . . . that cheap little judy didn't know anything about any crimes except running out with our winnings, you can bet on that."

"He's making the whole thing up, then?"

"Of course he is. I came after my money, yes, that's fair enough, and I wasn't particular how I went about recovering it, either, if it comes to that. But he'll have a hell of a job connecting me with that girl's death, or that gun he's raving about."

"Will I?" shrilled the vengeful voice from the kitchen, whinnying with triumph and whimpering with pain. "You think you're in the clear because you wiped off the grip nicely? Who loaded it in the first place, mate, think about that! Wait until they get their little insufflators on that magazine before you crow too loud."

Bunty closed her fingers excitedly on Luke's arm. And Fleet laughed. A little too loudly, perhaps; there seemed suddenly to be a bleak, small hollow inside the laughter, that echoed like a bare cell.

"Come off it, man! You know as well as I do I opened the thing up here to-night, here in this room, to see how many rounds were in it. You watched me do it! Like all the rest of the boys, and they'll all swear to it."

"You think so? This time you don't own all the witnesses, Fleet. At the best it'll be a draw, three-three. And by the time they've got it through their thick heads that you're going down for twenty years, you think you'll even be owning three of 'em? They won't be able to shift over to our side fast enough."

"You talk too much to be feeling sure of yourself," Fleet said tolerantly, and beamed at the inspector with a face of brass. But was there a very faint flare of uneasiness far down in the wells of his eyes? "You won't get far on his uncorroborated word," he said virtuously, "he's got a record as long as your arm. I don't know why I ever risked taking him on, but somebody has to give the lags a chance."

"A bit of corroboration would certainly be helpful," agreed the inspector reasonably. "Even on one specific point . . . say these trial letters she was supposed to be compiling, now. But of course, you deny there ever were any, and he says you burned them. In either case, nobody else is going to be able to give us any fresh information now." He was gently unfolding the sheet of thick white paper he had withdrawn from the envelope. He took his time about it, and its texture, or some quality he found in it, seemed to be affording him a certain obscure amusement. They observed that he handled it only by the edges, with considerable care. "Of course, if we could have called the girl herself as a witness . . ."

He looked up, smiling. "Now isn't that a coincidence! She had it among her papers, all ready stamped and addressed for posting, I suppose she was going to slip it into the box at London Airport at the last moment. No point in taking risks until she was actually on her way out. It's a good surface, it should hold prints well."

He turned it for them to see the sliced-out words and phrases of print from which it had been compiled.

"You want to know how the text reads? It's addressed to Superintendent Duckett, Chief of the Midshire C.I.D. It runs:

'The man you want for the Armitage hold-up is Jerome Fleet, who has the chain of garages that just opened a branch in Comerford. He uses his business for cover and transport. He has a man named Blackie Crowe working for him, also one called Skinner, and Sam Quilley, and a young one they call Con. They were all in the wage-snatch, and they did the fur job, too. I am not sure about his new manager, but think all his men except the locals are crooks. *But Fleet is the boss.*'

" Underlined, that last bit. And she signed herself, not too originally : ' A Well-Wisher '."

He looked up across the paper as he refolded it, and smiled into the amber eyes of a caged tiger. " Isn't it lucky, Mr. Fleet, that the fair copy survived?"

The moment of flat silence was broken abruptly by an outburst of loud, rattling, jarring sound from the kitchen, fed by gulping indrawn breaths of pain. It took them a few shocked seconds to realise that it was only Quilley, laughing.

CHAPTER XIV

IN THE BACK of the police car, speeding south down the A.73 south of Cumbernauld New Town, Bunty and Luke sat all but silent, shoulder to shoulder as on the white wicker settee in Louise Alport's devastated living-room.

"How am I ever going to face the Alports?" Luke had said, looking round his battle-field despairingly from the weary vantage-point of victory. " Louise will kill me !" So soon do words resume their normal easy and unthinking meaning. And Bunty had consoled him. " They'll forgive you ! On this story they can dine out for life !"

"Your husband's on the line, Mrs. Felse," said the driver. " He's through Kendal now, it won't be long. We'll run off and rendezvous with him at Lockerbie." And to the radio he said cheerfully : " You know the King's Arms, in High Street? They've got no parking space, but at this hour there'll be room in the street."

"He'll find it," said Bunty.

"You want to speak to him, Mrs. Felse?"

"Just give him my love," she said.

"Your boy's coming on now, ma'am. He says you cost him twenty-two bob for flowers, and they'll be dead before you see them."

"Tell him half a bottle of Cognac would have kept better."

"He says no Cognac, but there's a bottle of Riccadonna Bianca, though you don't deserve it."

She laughed, and her eyes gushed tears suddenly and briefly. Luke had never seen her in tears. There was always a new snare, a fresh, impossible attraction. Of course, they were crazy for her, those two men of hers rushing north to meet her because waiting was impossible. There would never be anyone like her, never, never, never. And now there wasn't much time left for him, he could feel the minutes slipping through his fingers like sand, and there was so much to say, so much that he wanted to say properly before he lost her for ever, so much he knew would never be said. There was the police driver, sitting there in front of them impersonal and incurious, but human. And nothing must ever be said of love, however love crowded his thoughts and made his heart faint.

It was enough, in a way, that she had invited him to go south with her. Naturally she was free to go, and naturally she wanted to reach her family as soon as possible, and return home with them; but he had still certain charges hanging over him, and he could have been held, had not she expressly asked to have him with her, and even punctiliously invited him to go with her, as if he could deny her anything, as if he would willingly have parted with her a moment sooner than he needed. It was enough because it meant that what had happened between them had a validity of its own, present and eternal, for her as well as for him. And in the car, between their few exchanges, she had slept confidingly against his shoulder, even nestled into the shelter of his diffident arm, and settled her cheek against his breast. The journey north, with death on his back and a gun in his hand ready for her, was only twenty-four hours past.

"I could stay," he said haltingly. "In Lockerbie, I mean. There'd surely be a room for me, this time of year. I mean, you'll want . . . your family . . . they'll want you to themselves. . . ."

"Don't be silly!" said Bunty warmly. "You're coming with us. Didn't I say I wasn't going home till I could take you with me?"

"I'm not much of a trophy," he said, and could not keep all the bitterness out of his tone.

"You're *not* a trophy. You're my co-victor. Without you there's no triumph, and I need a triumph. My family are very critical."

"I can imagine," he said, racked with unwilling laughter. And in a moment, very seriously indeed: "You know there are still several counts against me."

"I don't think anybody's going to be interested in throwing the book at you now," she said, yawning into his sleeve like a sleepy child. "Not after what we're bringing them." It still turned his heart over in a transport of joy and humility when she said "we."

"I don't mind. I shan't complain. Bunty," he said shyly, "you're happy, you've got everything. Why were you sad? When you came into the 'Orion', why were you so sad?"

She looked back at that moment with some astonishment, it seemed now so alien and so far away.

"Sometimes being happy doesn't seem enough. I was alone, and I'd stopped being young, and suddenly I didn't know where I was going or what I was for. It was you," she said, without calculation, "who cured me."

"I did? But I . . . I don't see," he said, trembling, "how *I* can have been much comfort or reassurance to you!"

"I didn't *want* to be comforted or reassured! I wanted

to be *used*! You had a use for me. *Me*! Not my husband's
wife or my son's mother. Me, Bunty!"

She felt his helpless adoration in the devoted stillness of
his body and the agonised tenderness of the arm that held
her, and she thought: Poor Luke! No, lucky Luke!
Everything rounded off firmly and finally for him, no let-
downs afterwards, no waking up gradually to the fact that
I'm nearly old enough to be his mother, and it's beginning
to show more grossly every year. No rejections, and no dis-
illusionments. Here he has me for ever. And for ever—no,
not young, perhaps, but never more than forty-one! And
brave and loyal and good, everything he wants to believe
me. When I need that reference to forward to the gods, I
shall know where to apply.

"All my life," she said, inspired, "I shall remember
you and be grateful to you."

And he, who had all this time been crying in his heart
how he would remember her always, and with eternal
gratitude and love, was so disarmed and so perfectly ful-
filled by her taking the words out of his heart that he never
missed the word she had omitted. So that it did not matter,
in the end, that she should wonder whether she had done
well to avoid the mention of love. It was not the only word
in the language; and as one of the most misused, it was
thankful, now and again, for reticence and silence.

: :   : :

She was asleep in his arm when the car ran off the dual
carriage-way and wound its way into the small, handsome
town, half asleep at the end of Sunday. The car from the
south was there before them, Luke saw the two men standing beside it, heads up, eyes alertly roving, waiting for them
to arrive. In the beam of headlights the two faces burned
out of the darkness eager, intent, impatient, as was only
proper when they were waiting for Bunty; and as the car
that brought her to them slipped smartly into a vacant
parking spot beside the kerb, Luke saw them both smooth
away the residue of wild anxiety out of their eyes, and the

tension of longing out of their faces. There is a certain
duty to take old love easily, even when it scalds.

Luke put a finger under Bunty's chin and gently raised
her face, and she awoke with eyes wide open, and smiled
at him as if he had always been there, and then, remembering, grew grave, because she knew he wasn't going to be
there much longer. She had too much sense to try to
turn him into a family friend, or even offer him a bed for
the night in the house where she belonged to someone else.
No, he would go, and not look back; he was wise, too.
And even for her it was going to be a kind of amputation,
another little death.

"Wake up," said Luke, "we're here in Lockerbie. And
look who's waiting for you."

She looked, and there was George already leaning to
open the door of the car for her, and his smile was muted,
indulgent and a shade superior, the smile every married
man keeps for the unpredictable idiot who lives somewhere within his sensible wife. Marriage is a round-dance
as well as a sacrament.

Bunty slid her feet out to the pavement, and stepped into
her husband's arms, as simply as if he had been meeting her
train after a shopping expedition to London. This is how
it's done, Luke thought, watching. If you're clever, this is
how it's done. The panic being over, and the fear gone,
why exclaim? Why startle and shake the assured equili-
brium of a relationship on which the foundations of three
lives rest? And why express what is already known, valued,
impregnable? Not to say inexpressible! No affectation, no
fuss, no explanations. If they ever talked about the fearful
truths of that week-end it would be afterwards, in tran-
quillity, walking softly to shake no hearts. But it did not
mean that the hearts had not been shaken. Luke saw
George's face over his wife's shoulder, as he held her briefly
in his arms, and there was no question after that of Bunty
being under-valued. George knew what he'd got, all
right.

re a fine one," he said, kissing her roundly. "So
n't mix with dangerous types who carry guns! Talk
t famous last words!"

She kissed him back joyfully. "Did you have a nice
trip, dear?" she said wickedly.

"No, I did not!" He took his hands from her slowly.
Their delight in her wholeness cried aloud, and their re-
luctance to relinquish her even to Dominic, who stood
waiting his turn. "My man was a dead loss. A perfectly
respectable person who didn't know him has put him miles
away from our job. And the next thing I knew, Dom was
on the line demanding to know what I'd done with *you*."

"It's all in the family," said Bunty largely. "You don't
have to go on north to pick up the pieces, do you?"

"No. This one Duckett's finishing off himself. My only
orders are to take you two safely home."

Bunty turned to offer her cheek for Dominic's dutiful
kiss. The boy—he was absurdly like her—was less practised
in carrying the burden. He hugged her fiercely all the time
he was saying, in his best throw-away manner: "Many
happy returns of yesterday, Mummy! How was the fishing?" The hazel eyes, the image of her own, were devouring her hungrily and jealously with every word, but the
voice was all right.

"You mean it's *still* Sunday? It seems to have lasted for
ever."

Luke had got out of the car, and was standing well back
from a ceremony in which he conceived he had no part.
But it seemed that Bunty thought differently, for she
turned back to him, smiling, holding George by the hand.

"And here's Luke. He's heading home for Comerbourne, too, the police had to hang on to his car for the
time being."

Luke never wanted to see that car again, though he had
loved it in its time. When it was released he would get some
dealer to remove it, and get rid of it, perhaps even forget it
some day.

" You won't mind if Luke and I collar the back seat, will you?" said Bunty, looking appreciatively at the large black police car George had borrowed for the sake of its radio. " We haven't had much rest over the week-end, we're probably going to sleep all the way home."

We! God bless her for that " we " that bound him to her even now, for the little while they had left before normality set in.

" Hallo, Luke!" said George gravely. "You seem to have been doing my job for me . . . even to bringing my wife back safely. Thank you!"

Luke looked from the smiling dark face to the two linked hands, that fitted together with so much passion and so deep a calm, and he suddenly saw in them the whole essence of this marriage, no, of marriage entire. He thought it would be worth waiting and hunting through half a lifetime to find another hand that would fit into his like that.

When he shook hands with George, it was like touching Bunty again, they were so deeply one. What Bunty had given to Luke he couldn't begin to appraise. What they gave him now between them was a dazzling promise. It seemed this union was possible. If it had happened once, it could happen again. Even in this measure. Even, some day, to him?

::   ::

Bunty awoke towards morning with a soft, alarmed cry of : " Luke!" stretching out her arm protectively over George's wakeful body. All night he had lain beside her and watched her exhausted sleep, and learned by heart, even in moderate moonlight, the shadows that marked her face, the memories of things lived through and still not put away. He could wait; he must wait. She had told no more than the half, the rest she would tell when the right time came. He cupped her cheek in his hand and soothed her fully awake, to end her distress.

She folded her arm over him more closely, caressing his

...d even in the darkness of his shoulder he felt her

... love you!" she said in a deep sigh. There are times
... mention love, as there are times to take it for granted,
and keep silent.

"Did you love *him*," said George gently, stroking back
the tangled brown hair from her forehead.

"It depends," said Bunty after due thought, "on what
you mean by love."

This is an acid test, if ever there was one. Forget the
narrow, deep confines of marriage, so exclusive and so profound, and what *do* you mean by love?

"I mean," said George, moistening his lips in awe,
"whatever it is that makes it possible to achieve a complete
human contact with another person, maybe only for three
minutes on a crowded bus. I mean the thing, whatever it
is, that suddenly makes you move in on somebody else's
need, and strike clean through conventions into their hearts,
so that there'll always be a link between you, even if you
never meet or even think of each other again. I mean the
communicated warmth that keeps people alive, the most
universal and generous thing there is, not the narrowest.
Not sexual love, not married love, not platonic love, not
filial love, nothing that has to be qualified—the absolute.
I mean *love*, love!"

She lay beside him for a long while in stillness and
silence, he began to think she had fallen asleep again, and
this time without dreams. But presently she turned to him
impulsively, and wound her arm about him with a sharp,
sweet sigh of fulfilment, and embraced him with all her
might.

"Then, yes," said Bunty, "I loved him."